the Shadowman

MARK BROWNLESS

ISBN-10: 1093368895
ISBN-13: 978-1093368895

The Shadow Man comes out at night
The Shadow Man in plain sight
The Shadow Man is gone by dawn
Taking souls for us to mourn

The Shadow Man prowls around
Without noise, without a sound
And if he should catch your eye
Then you know you're going to die

The Shadow Man haunts our home
You're safe until the sun goes down
The Shadow Man will wait his turn
To hold you close and make you burn

HE CAME BACK FROM THE OTHER SIDE
NOW THE OTHER SIDE WANTS HIM BACK

THE
HAND
OF
AN
ANGEL

MARK BROWNLESS

AVAILABLE NOW FROM AMAZON

Chapter 1

– Now –

Funny Things

They're funny things, childhood memories.

You remember a house as huge when it's an average size, or a long cycle ride that's just around the corner. Maybe it's because you were smaller when the memories were formed, and so, as a grown-up, you're just, well, bigger. But that doesn't explain why you always remember childhood summers as long and hot. They weren't. They weren't any different to now. You just edit out the rain.

I couldn't remember anything about the summer of 1985, when I was fifteen, apart from watching Live Aid in a static caravan, and my uncle calling Sting, *Stink*, and me pleading to be able to stay up to watch the American bit. And watching *Alien* for the first time – on the telly – and how I nearly shat myself when the beast had a sudden close-up with that extendable jaw. And shielding a little kid called Scott from a ram that had escaped from a nearby field and getting butted really hard in the thighs.

That was all. Nothing else in the tank. Until last week, when I had the dream again. It was a dream I hadn't thought about for thirty years, and then it just appeared. Like that, for no reason. The day after the email. But nothing happens without a reason, and now things are starting to come back.

Like us out on our bikes all summer long, marauding around the villages and the countryside, getting into 'bother' as my mum used to call it. Like skinny-dipping at the lake – *our* lake. Like being free – like the feeling that we could do anything, and nothing could stop us.

Except something did.

Someone.

And as I had the dream, the dream of us singing the nursery rhyme – the scariest fucking nursery rhyme that's passed my lips – I had this thought, this image in my head, of a body. I had the idea that something had started again. Something I had no recollection of. Something that had happened before.

Another burning.

And I knew that I had to go back. To Janey.

Memories.

You just can't trust 'em.

Chapter 2

— Now —

Coming Home

I lay in the darkness. Cocooned. Cushioned by my mattress, enveloped by the softness of my duvet. I tried to change position, but my arms were pinned to my sides. Panicking, I tried to sit up, but I was held in place. I opened my eyes and stared at the moon above, shining brightly in the clear night sky. I wasn't in my bed at all but rather in a shallow grave, the hole just wide enough to fit, covered in soil to keep me in place, with just my head exposed. In my nose and throat was the acrid stench of mud and shit and decay and death, which became increasingly overpowering so that I almost gagged. And then something crawled over me. Something big, something insectoid or reptilian, yet human all the same.

I started to sing a nursery rhyme, something I knew would protect me, something we'd sung when we were afraid and thought it would come to get us. I sang it through a dry mouth and chattering teeth, stifling sobs at the end of each line.

It crawled across the bodies of the others lying beside me, then it was above me, on top of me, holding itself up on its arms like a lover. The sigh of its rotten breath was one of despair. It hung over me, eyes staring deep into my soul, scouring back through every past life, my heart hammering in my chest, threatening to break through. The sickly stench grew as its face neared mine, about to deliver whatever killing blow it would use to drag me to hell.

I sat upright in bed, stifling a cry, taking a big deep breath instead. I was drenched in sweat. I got up, dumping my soaking pyjamas in the washing basket and getting a fresh t-shirt from the airing cupboard. At least I hadn't woken Nick or the kids.

This was the fourth night running I'd had the dream and I needed a good night's sleep, ready for a long drive tomorrow.

Going home.

Funny how it still felt like that after all these years. But now it seemed very different, like it was a whole different place. Now the dreams were back.

'Philippa Henstridge.' I pushed the hands-free button on the steering wheel.

'We've gotta do something about the Kettering account.'

'Morning to you too, Giles. Why isn't your number coming up on my phone?'

'Because I'm in the office, of course,' replied Giles, sounding flustered. I imagined him in his round, wire-framed glasses, denim shirt and corduroy jacket.

'Oh okay, sure.'

'They've been on this morning, wanting you and only you, except you appear to be not here.'

'Yeah. Jan knows. Family emergency.'

'You haven't got any family.'

'Extended family emergency, then. Bit of a strange one, really. Will explain all when I get back. I need to take a couple of days.'

'A couple of days – what do I tell Kettering? They're going fucking schitz.'

'What do you tell them, or what'd you like to tell them?'

'Don't be flippant.'

'If I couldn't be flippant, I might as well be dead. Tell them Maxine and Dave are taking a specialist pass over the file, giving the campaign a further polish above and beyond what I've done. We'll get it to them midweek next. In fact, tell them this is part of a brand-new platinum service we've been developing the last few months and we're piloting it with them at no extra charge.'

'I can't believe you.'

'I'm bloody good, aren't I?'

If only I was.

∞ ∞ ∞

Lincolnshire was flat. I mean, really flat, like twinned-with-rural-Holland-flat. But around us, around Laurendon, the village where I spent the first eighteen years of my life, it was a little more rolling. Laurendon itself had a big hill in the middle and could be seen from miles around. Like a tit, we used to say when we were kids, and as I curved around the fifty mile-an-hour left-hander and saw the village on the hill a mile away, that's what I thought of. Of course, the village grew out from the hill, spreading out onto flatter land, which was where we'd lived. It made me smile to remember what a chore it was to go and call on friends who lived at altitude. I'm not saying we were lazy, but I was always glad most of my friends didn't live up the hill.

Less than a week on from the first dream and the memories of that summer are lifting out of the fog like one of those 3D pictures – the music, the fashion, the weather, and the things we'd done. But there were still holes in there. Things that didn't sit right. How could I remember something, seemingly so well, and yet have some complete holes right next to it? And worse still, they weren't holes I *knew* I couldn't remember – like what I did at a party when I was drunk. They were like a black hole, invisible, like I'd never experienced them – I just knew there was something missing. And now I thought about it, what was missing must be something glaringly obvious, as if I'd built a pink fence around it and hung it with hundreds of fairy lights.

What didn't I know? And why had I forgotten it?

I'd bought the '80s Hits' CD in a motorway services on a whim, and played it all the rest of the way back. It felt like I needed some kind of connection to the old place to make me feel at home again, but Duran Duran were currently doing a reasonable job of making me think of Rio.

The dream had created this strong atmosphere of back then, the feeling of that summer, evoking images and even smells that were familiar, but were suddenly blown out of the water by what happened at the end. One repeating dream. The dream of the lake, the foreboding, the smell of rot and fear. Then there was the Shadow Man, and the nursery rhyme. The song we'd created to keep us safe, the song that I'd not thought of in thirty years. And there was Janey. Janey, who'd emailed me after all this time, the day before the first dream.

But Janey always was the fire starter.

I drove along the straight mile 'two-lane black top' as the Americans would call it, heading toward Laurendon. The road undulated wildly, bouncing the car around much more than I remembered, and I wondered just how badly you could lay tarmac. I went round the corner and entered the village, turning left immediately into Stow Lane. There were several cars parked outside Janey's bungalow.

Janey's bungalow!

She'd told me in emails that it was hers now her parents had died, but in my mind it still felt like her parents' place, that apparently she hadn't set foot outside of since… then. But what was 'then'? She'd stayed at home for thirty years and not left, because of something I knew but couldn't remember. This whole memory thing was really starting to piss me off.

The bungalow had seen better days. It didn't look like Janey had done too much with the place after her parents had passed, but why would you, if you never went outside? The paint on the windows had long since blistered and peeled, the walls were grey when they were once brilliant white. A small greenhouse was a rotting glassless skeleton just past the side porch, and the faded, wheel-less remains of a kid's pedal car – Janey's pedal car – guarded the front of the garage.

I wasn't sure what to expect when I knocked on the uPVC porch door. In some ways I expected old-Janey to appear, almost forgetting how different I looked compared with then. But then old-Janey did appear; the same straight brown hair falling awkwardly beyond her shoulders with a centre parting, the same waif-like physique and hollow posture. Closer inspection did reveal new things – wrinkles and crow's feet, strands of grey hair in amongst the brown, the makings of an extra chin.

We were all that much older.

'Well, well, Philippa Dover. Or rather, Mrs Henstridge I should say.'

'Janey Pullman,' I smiled at her and pulled her into an embrace. She stiffened as I put my arms around her, almost as if it was painful. She didn't hug back.

Janey led me into the lounge, which was a faded version of what I remembered; the red patterned carpet, now almost threadbare, the three-piece suite of brown leather, cracked and split, and the old mahogany TV unit in the corner, with thankfully a more modern screen than the old wooden-clad black and white TV her folks had when I'd first met them. Yet it seemed just like old times, and there were the others, although between us we did seem to fill the room more than we had back then. No Sally Chen for the moment, but here were Katie Edwards, Clarabelle

Walker, Janey and me. We exchanged awkward hugs and air kisses – none of us knowing how to really say hello.

'I can't believe we're all here. Especially because, well, don't take this the wrong way, but I haven't even thought about you lot in, like, thirty years,' I said with genuine surprise.

'How do you not take that the wrong way?' asked Katie with mock offence.

'I haven't thought about you guys either,' added Clara.

'Of course you haven't,' replied Janey, the slightest of sneers in her voice.

'Oh?'

'It's because we've all forgotten.'

'Well no shit, Sherlock. Course we've forgotten, it was a long time ago.'

'It's because we were made to forget,' she added, taking the floor.

'Hang on a minute, can't we wait for the kettle to boil?' Clara asked.

'Made to? By whom?' Katie responded.

'It's like Katie said, it was just a long time ago, that's all, and it's not like we're getting any younger,' Clara added.

'But you all had a dream last week, right?' Janey asked.

'I probably had a few…'

'Don't be obtuse, Katie, you know exactly which dream I'm talking about,' Janey said icily. Everyone went quiet. We knew.

'Yes, the dreams have started again, just like before.' It was a simple statement, but I needed to say it as confirmation, to get everyone on the same page. I'd intended it to start us talking but we all sat in silence. Nobody played coy. Nobody threw in a 'what dreams, hun?' It seemed like we were already beyond that. 'You've all had them too, then? The dreams we had back then, after that summer..?'

'I did, it was horrible – down by the lake trapped in dirt and disgusting smells and someone... terrible,' said Clara.

'It was back then, that summer.' I looked at my old school friends as I spoke. 'Riding around on our bikes, going out to the lake, but it was scary. Something was there, watching from the shadows. It tried to do something to us, and we sang that song – the nursery rhyme we made up. I hadn't thought about it in all this time.'

'Nobody had, right? And you all had the same dream?' Janey smiled triumphantly.

'I did,' Katie answered.

'Oh, fuck off!' Clarabelle hadn't changed. 'People can't all just have the same dream!'

'I had it too, that's why I emailed you.' Janey looked at each of us in turn.

'Hang on, I started having the dreams *after* your email, Janes. That means you must've started having the dreams before us?' I looked at her for confirmation and she nodded. 'For how long?'

'A couple of weeks, maybe – I'm not sure.'

'I had my first one after you emailed as well,' Katie said.

'Okay, me too,' Clara admitted.

'So why were you the lucky girl, Janey, why did the dreams come to you before us?' Katie raised her eyebrows and crossed her eyes to make the early exchanges of our visit seem less like an interrogation.

'I don't know – I've been trying to work that out. Maybe it's because I never left. I'm more connected to this place, perhaps. I've had some odd dreams down the years that kind of hinted of things that happened back then, but nothing like the ones I've had recently.'

'What was your dream?' I asked, assuming she would've had the same as everyone else.

'It was in the desert, I'm flying over the dunes, going some, like a missile. And I come upon this circle of people, surrounded by fire, and there's this dark figure in the middle.'

'Bloody hell,' said Katie.

'Yes, but it doesn't end there. The figure is darkness itself and then I'm down there in the circle of people and he surrounds us and suddenly there are flames, and they all close in, people bursting into flames. And then I wake up.'

'So different to us then?'

'I'm quite amazed you've all dreamt the same thing. . I think even if the stimulus was the same, your interpretation is always going to be different. When I first had the dream, it took me back to then, and I started to remember things. Things that were different to how I remembered. So I started tracking you down – took a little while, but I'm pretty resourceful. I needed to know if you'd had them too, to see if you were okay,' Janey winked her one good eye at us.

'What did you mean when you said we'd been made to forget?' I asked, a good deal more uncomfortable than when I'd arrived. The damp, stuffy bungalow felt several degrees colder.

'I stayed. I haven't left this house let alone the village, so I've forgotten less.'

'What does *that* mean?' asked Katie.

'It means I know more than you do, stupid. It means I wondered if you'd been having the dreams, too. It means maybe whatever was making us forget has stopped, or changed or something.'

'You mean, like the 'spell' would get broken?' said Katie, using her finger to make speech marks around *spell*. 'And don't call me stupid.'

'Sorry. I didn't say it was magic or anything, either. But something made you all totally forget what happened that summer – that whole year before we left school for that matter. And it's only just starting to come back, isn't it? You couldn't remember the first time you got fingered until last week.' Janey was pacing around the middle of the room now, holding court, limping heavily on her prosthesis, the hinged knee clicking with every step. 'You can think I'm fucked up, that I'm a mess for being like I am, for staying here in this house and not moving, for getting in contact. But the one thing you can't explain is why you forgot an important chunk of your life until last week.'

'Hang on, I didn't say I couldn't remember parts of my life,' I said. 'Just that I had different memories.'

'But you couldn't though, right?' I sat and stared at Janey – I had no answer for her. 'Important parts of your growing up and all you can remember is a two-dimensional picture and that's it.'

'Bad stuff happened that summer, didn't it?' Clara asked, rhetorically.

'Yes,' said Janey. 'I think so. I haven't pieced it together yet.'

'People died, right?'

'Yes, I think so.'

'Wait, I've just remembered something,' Katie said, almost an air of excitement about her. 'It's a name: Ethel Grimshaw.'

'Old lady Grimshaw. I remember her,' I added for the record.

'Anyone get what happened to her yet?' Janey asked.

'Hang on, didn't she burn to death?' said Clara.

∞ ∞ ∞

The lounge was twilight dark as the dirty blinds stayed permanently closed. It was stuffy and damp-smelling, and almost… something else. Like the smell of despair. On the table in the corner was an old chunky laptop and a pile of books – mainly horror fiction. I excused myself to go and use the bathroom.

I walked down the hallway, shocked at the memories it brought back from thirty years before, with the brown wood veneer cladding, the fake wood skirting boards and faded tatty pictures on the walls. I glanced into Janey's parents' room and it looked like it hadn't been touched – as if the bed had been made by her mum on the day she died and had been left alone since. Janey hadn't moved rooms. Her door was open, too, and I paused, looking in. I could hear the others talking in the sitting room. Janey's bedroom was chaotic, with clothes and sheets of paper scattered around the floor, the curtains drawn creating shadows everywhere. She had a battered *Star Wars* mobile above her chest of drawers and a globe lamp that had clearly had an accident at one point because most of Europe was missing, the bulb shining out harshly through the Northern Hemisphere. Hundreds of overlapping newspaper cut-outs and pictures were pinned like a collage to a large noticeboard on the back wall, like some seventies police investigation. A black trilby hung on the corner of the cork board, a black scarf draped over it. The globe lamp did little to cut through the gloom, but I could see a small table in front, on it was a papier-mâché model of a landscape, which I couldn't quite place. I glanced over my shoulder and saw no one in the hall. The others were still talking in the lounge. I walked into the room to get a closer look, stepping over Janey's underwear and dinner dishes, the shiny disc in the centre was suddenly the lake and there were the trees around it and the grassy banks, exactly as I remembered them, exactly as they'd been in the dream. It was a poor, childish model but it hit me like a punch in the face. I was transported there, standing on the bank looking out across the water, the warm wind in my hair and the happy shouts and screams of my friends forming the soundtrack. Then the screams and shouts sounded less content, and more like they were afraid.

There were dolls in the basin of the lake.

She's nearly fifty and she's playing with dolls?

Janey had made a doll for each of us. There was her own of course, with her burns and her leg – that must've taken some adapting. There was Katie with her freckles and her wild auburn hair – the freckles looked drawn on, with eyeliner, maybe. This was too weird. Clara's avatar was there with Sal's and so was mine. Fuck it was creepy. I left the room quickly before I was caught snooping around, and re-joined the others after doing what I needed to do.

'So what's going on, Janey?' I said. 'Why'd you start dreaming again? Why now?'

'Yeah, has anything happened round here?' Katie asked.

'Nothing ever happens around here.' Janey smiled slightly for the first time since we'd arrived. She could almost look pretty when she did, almost lost the haunted expression she always seemed to carry. The smile lifted her face. It lifted half of her face, that is. The whorled discoloured scarring on the other side barely shifted. So her almost-pretty smile was a sneer.

'Yeah, but does it, though?' I knew I had to push her to get anywhere, always had to. With a delicate touch you could actually have an open conversation.

'I don't think so. I don't hear anything. I… I don't go out,' the right side of her face flushed. 'Or see anyone.' She looked like a frightened little girl now.

'But don't you get any gossip?'

Janey shook her head. 'The only direct interaction I have is with the Tesco delivery driver each week. And the Amazon guy, of course.'

'Christ.' I looked across at the table. 'You got wi-fi?'

'Yes of course, I'm a recluse, not Amish. There's my laptop.' Janey went across to her small desk in the corner of the room and opened her computer. She booted up Google and looked at me for direction. Nothing changes. I asked her to call up the local paper, *The Enquirer*.

'Someone's burned to death. There's your answer, kiddo, right there.' I read from the article. 'Louise Jordan was found in her bedroom, burned beyond recognition, leaving only her foot, forearms and half her head intact, the rest burnt to ash. There was no sign of an intruder, or of arson, so initial conclusions are that Ms Jordan died accidentally. The forensic fire team concluded that there was no evidence of an accelerant, no trigger in the form of a cigarette or spark, so they have listed the cause as unknown'.'

'Spontaneous human combustion?' asked Katie, quietly.

'Yes, that's it, that's what was going on back then! Wasn't it? So it's happening again. Fuck. Just like thirty years ago?' Clara wasn't really asking, and almost seemed excited to have remembered something.

'But this sort of thing just doesn't happen – scientists have disproved it –'

'Well, they've disproved some aspects, but if someone goes up like this, what else could it be?' Janey interrupted Katie before she could go any further.

'And you think this links to whatever happened back then?' Katie continued.

'What else can it be? These things never happen in such a concentrated area. It's the only explanation.'

'And then there are the dreams. You had the dreams first. D'you think that whatever it was that made us forget everything is making us dream again and maybe…' I indicated the screen, 'doing this?'

'Yeah, look, I don't know any more than you do and I'm sorry I got you involved with this. I just sent the email to see if you'd had the dream like I had. I didn't mean to get you to come back, but here you are. All I know is that something is wrong. Something must be very wrong if we're having the dreams again. But to answer your question, then yes, I do think that whatever did *this*,' she indicated her face and leg, 'is on its way back.'

'What makes you think that?' I asked, searching my memory banks for any recollection of what actually happened to Janey.

'I don't know. It's like a growing fear, or dread or something.' Janey shrugged.

'Do you remember the dream?' asked Katie. 'Do you remember how it ended?'

'Yes, it says that you can't tell your parents, or it'll come true.'

'Yes, but what was it? What was the thing?'

'You haven't remembered yet?' Janey seemed almost pleased to have the exclusive.

'Well, that much I do know – come on, hun, out with it.'

'The Shadow Man. We called it – it was called – the Shadow Man.'

The Shadow Man. I remembered it from my dream too, but had no idea what it was.

'You know that does sound familiar, now you mention it,' said Katie.

'More things are coming back to me, too,' I agreed. 'It's like the fog is clearing.'

'But it can't have been true, can it?' said Clara. 'What happened to Janey notwithstanding, there isn't a bogeyman! We're forty-five years old for God's sake. Do you still believe in monsters and demons?'

'No, course not!'

'So how is any of this real?'

Chapter 3

— Then —

Ethel Grimshaw

Ethel 'old lady' Grimshaw, also lived in a bungalow at the opposite end of Stow Lane, her back garden bordering the park. She was a mean old bastard. Nasty. Acerbic. She once threatened to kill Boxey, Janey's dog, when he got out of the garden and ended up barking at her from the street.

'Should be poisoned, yappy little monster,' she'd said. We were all so upset that Janey's dad went to speak to her. He never told us what she'd said, but I doubt she apologised. The funny thing was that Boxey did die a few weeks later. Janey never spoke about it, but he wasn't run over and he'd not been ill, so I guess I'll never know how he died – maybe Janey won't either, but, as The Christians once sang, *when the fingers point...*

Stow Lane was a long straight road, leading from Hadley Road, the main road through the village, to where it bisected Lake Road going out of the village and Coopers Lane going right by the pond. As kids it seemed like it was a mile long and we sometimes called it the straight mile – drag racing our bikes against each other along its length. When I got a milometer for my bike, we were all a bit surprised to find it was a little less than half that length. From one end to the other you could see the immaculately trimmed bushes and lawns of the homes it served – the small, sixties bungalows close to the road on the right, like Janey's place nearer the Hadley end, and the bigger, newer houses set back from the road with their big front gardens on the other side, nearer Coopers Lane. That morning, we'd been walking down to the park from Janey's, and had seen some vehicles outside Old Lady Grimshaw's bungalow – which was sandwiched, uncomfortably, between two of those big new houses – two police cars, an ambulance and a van, all with blue and red flashing lights disturbing the stillness of the sunny morning. A small group of middle-aged women stood brazenly staring at the house, whispering gossip to each other, and a policeman was standing at the foot of the drive to stop them getting any closer.

'What's happened?' I asked.

'Never you mind, miss, just be on your way,' the copper replied.

We walked past the house, craning our necks as people in blue overalls went in and out of the open front door.

'She's dead,' said Janey, matter-of-factly.

'Fuck off,' said Clara. 'How do you know? And if she is,' she added, thinking she was on a roll of being right, 'why is there an ambulance not a hearse?'

'Those are forensics people – they don't come into an old lady's house if she isn't dead. And they'd obviously have an ambulance to start with, just in case she wasn't.'

'Let's go round to the park and see what we can see from there!' Clara suggested.

'Yeah, good idea!' We all broke into a run, regretting that we hadn't brought our bikes, sprinting to the end of the road and round to the park entrance. We ran up the slope, along the tarmac path that took us along the end of the football pitch, with its bare patches of soil in the goalmouths bordered by rusted, net-less posts. The pitch markings had long since lost their white paint, but remained as deep burnt trenches, vying to catch an unwary ankle.

'Watch the crap!' I said, dodging a pile of what a dog-walker nowadays would carry home in a poop-sack. Clara didn't see the pile of shit until it was almost too late, reacting to avoid giving her new white Adidas trainers – *fake from the market* – a proper christening, she managed to land her feet either side of it, but her body carried on travelling at speed, and she went flying off the path, rolling over and over in the daisy-covered grass like a stunt man, tufts of grass and flower heads thrown up around her.

'You bellend!' We all laughed and carried on running, beyond the football pitch to the tennis courts – two full-sized courts of badly laid tarmac, buckled and warped in places with tufts of grass growing through. The two wooden vegetable crates we used to mark the net posts were in place as always, as if on guard. Mrs Grimshaw's garden bordered the hedge directly behind them and we'd often had to sneak through the hole in the broken chain-link fence, and push through the gap in the prickly, dense cotoneaster hedge to retrieve a ball. Just as often we'd be greeted by the venom in her tongue as she lay in wait for us.

Today was much more straightforward, we pushed through the hedge in single file, crawling on our hands and knees until we were lined up in her rose border, with neat rows of French marigolds and begonias before us, framing the small square of lawn. The bungalow had two large windows at the back, the kitchen on the right and her bedroom on the left. We ran in single file across the grass, bent double like paras on manoeuvres, heading straight for the kitchen window, poking our heads and hands up over the sill like chads to peer inside. The room was empty, her walking stick and tartan wheeled shopping trolley standing idle by the back door. We crabbed sideways to the bedroom and did our stealth looking again. And there she was, or at least, there was what was left of someone who might once have been Ethel Grimshaw.

It appeared that four limbs were randomly scattered around a large pile of ash that had once been her body in the middle of the bed. The lower parts of her limbs were completely untouched by the fire, as was half of her white nylon nightie – the large blue flowers still clearly visible. The rest of the room seemed perfectly normal, with no sign of smoke or charring from the flames. How could such an intense fire have consumed her and done so little damage to the room?

A blue-overalled figure walked in and instantly saw us gawping at the floor show. He was followed by a man in a cheap shiny suit – the kind you could see in Top Man or Burtons in town – he had a bushy moustache and thinning auburn hair combed over to the side of his head.

'Oi!' he shouted, but we were off, back across the lawn, through the hedge – much more quickly than on the way in – and into the park. We made a point of walking quietly toward the exit so as not to arouse suspicion, our hearts racing with the fear of being caught, although quite what we thought would happen even if they'd caught us I don't know – it's not like being nosey is a crime. As we left Old Lady Grimshaw's garden behind, I could hear the voices of police officers in the garden, looking for us, and so once again we ran, sprinting through the park as if our lives depended on it, as if the officers had abandoned their investigations and decided to give chase to us, just for the hell of it. We hurdled the faecal trainer magnets and sprinted for the exit, turning a sharp right out of the gate and heading past Sowerby's farm, running by the pond with Coopers Lane curving around it to the right and heading straight on up the hill on Brewery Road – which always struck me as odd as there'd never been a brewery in the village as far as anyone knew. We didn't stop until we'd cut through the back of the woods and run the mile or so to Clarabelle's, still half expecting to hear the sound of approaching sirens. We sat on her low garden wall panting heavily, surrounded by a collection of planters and hanging baskets all lit-up with vibrant reds and blues, their heady scent making us feel queasy as we tried to get our breath back, red-faced, both exhilarated and revulsed at the same time.

'Fuck. Did you see the state of her?' Clarabelle was the first to say something.

'Christ there were bits of her all over the place,' said Katie.

'No, there was just her on the bed.'

'I know what I saw, Janey, her arms and legs were just scattered on the bed.'

'No, there was just no middle bit.'

'What?'

'Her body was gone – that was the pile of ash – leaving all the rest as if her body had disappeared or something.'

'And fire did that?' I asked.

'Yeah, what else?' Janey was quite dismissive.

'I meant, why didn't the rest of the room go up – why just the middle bit of her? How can fire be so selective?'

'Dunno, looked pretty fucking bizarre to me.'

Over the next few days we were glued to news reports about Mrs Grimshaw's death. It didn't become big news at first; an old lady died – stop the press. The local news aired a story saying she'd been burned to death but the fire investigators couldn't determine the cause of the blaze, or why all of her hadn't been consumed. Pictures from her bedroom were leaked to a newspaper, so the images we'd seen through the window were now there for all to see. With no ideas of their own, and no easy way to create some closure, the Press turned to external sources for an angle. The BBC found their own expert in forensics and he suggested a number of reasons why Mrs Grimshaw's body might have burned like it did. Then ITV found Professor Johnny Lankham. He was described as an expert in unexplained phenomenon, and particularly in spontaneous human combustion. He was a bit of a rock star – tightly curled wiry hair, wraparound glasses with a check shirt and knitted tie, he looked like the love-child of Art Garfunkel and Bono who'd gone on to become a geography teacher. Prof Johnny loved the camera, and ITV loved him, and he became the go-to guy for all things bizarre or strange. A television magazine show had found him at the University of Manchester, where he lectured in Sociology but was fairly outspoken in his other specialty in the local press, and in various publications and speaking engagements. They interviewed him on campus, but he was so newsworthy for this story, they brought him to Laurendon. He appeared on the corner of Hadley Road and Stow Lane and did part of an interview, the rest of which was filmed outside Mrs Grimshaw's house and by the pond.

'So, Professor Lankham, can you confirm that this lady burned to death in … unusual circumstances?'

'Yes, Shona, I can. Mrs Ethel Grimshaw was asleep in her bed, when, for reasons unknown at this stage, her body ignited, burning it to ash, yet, mysteriously, leaving her limbs almost untouched.' He said 'mysteriously' with raised hands and eyes wide, like a magician at a kids' birthday party, aiming to ramp up the mystery of his act. He was certainly captivating Shona McIntyre, the presenter.

'Is there any evidence of foul play in this case, in your opinion?'

'No, not at all, this is a classic case of spontaneous human combustion, where, for reasons unknown, people burst into flames.'

'Why do you think it was that only Mrs Grimshaw's body was consumed by the flames, yet her arms and legs weren't?'

'That's a good question, Shona, and one which has puzzled science for hundreds of years in these cases. There is a famous case of a man whose torso was completely incinerated yet his legs remained unscathed, and there have been others, typically sitting in a chair, who will just leave a pile of ash but limbs intact.' The news piece cut between the interview and old stock footage of burnt bodies to illustrate his point.

'So the fire centres around the body of the person only?'

'Yes, in the majority of cases, it does.'

'Why is that – do theories exist?'

'There are a number. Some investigators have hypothesised that victims might have been alcoholics, with so much alcohol in their gut that it has ignited and burnt them from within but not touched the periphery of their bodies. Others have suggested a 'wicking' effect of cigarettes and maybe alcohol combined, creating a slow burn that gradually consumes parts of the victim but leaves other parts unscathed, such as the limbs as we've seen here.'

∞ ∞ ∞

I picked up the phone after watching the show. Some people had push button phones now, Clara even had a cordless one, but not us, no, we had a regular old-fashioned avocado phone with a dial. I dialled Clara's number. As the phone rang I sat down in the hallway, having pulled the phone cord under the lounge door – not the easiest thing to do as Dad still hadn't got around to planing the bottom of the door off since the arrival of the new, thicker carpet nearly a year ago. Shutting the door took some effort.

'Did you see the news?' I asked as she answered, slightly out of breath.

'Yeah, the scientist guy.'

'So it was spontaneous human combustion…?'

'Fuck off. People don't just burst into flames – they just don't. And why wasn't her nightie or bed clothes burned too? Nah, something's not right. Well, apart from someone being dead not being right, of course.'

∞ ∞ ∞

For days, TV crews raced around the village trying to interview as many people as possible – anyone who'd ever spoken to Mrs Grimshaw, as we now more respectfully referred to her, now that she was dead. We watched all of this from the outside – occasionally they'd try and speak to us but we avoided them like the plague. They didn't know that we'd seen more of the case up close than anyone other than the police on the scene, and we could've told that story, but it didn't interest us. Besides, in the back of my mind I was still worried we'd get into trouble if they found out we'd been snooping in her garden. The naivety of youth. Instead we followed them, watching from afar, sitting on our bikes around a corner as herds of journalists migrated from one lead to the next.

Interest in the story started to wane after that. A few journalists did longer pieces about the village or Mrs Grimshaw – one particularly nasty piece of lazy journalism in the local paper ripped off Professor Lankham's interview and suggested that she'd had a drink problem and had fallen asleep pissed with a cigarette in her hand. Lankham stayed around for a couple of days, speaking in turn to both ITV and the BBC as well as the various freelance magazine journalists who'd stayed.

But gradually they drifted away, disappearing on the wind it seemed, until one day, after about a week, the village was ours again, and the vans and the cars and the cameras and the people holding sound booms and make-up brushes had all gone.

Chapter 4

— Now —

The Wheatsheaf

It wasn't long before Janey started to look tired. Emotionally exhausted from the events of the last week or two and from interacting with people for the first time in thirty years, but also from trying in her own way to play host and ply us with tea and soft cheesy biscuits. I suggested we decamp to the village pub where the rest of us were staying. Janey had offered to put some of us up at her place, but we'd politely made our excuses about arranging to stay in the village, and not wanting to be any trouble. More than that, though, Janey's was so dark, dusty and damp, it was already halfway to being a haunted house (bungalow), and nobody wanted to be anywhere near it. We did try to persuade her to join us for dinner later, but she repeatedly declined. I could tell she was pleased to be asked, almost enjoying being part of a group again, blushing and being bashful when we ribbed her. But she wasn't yet ready to take the next step to going outside her door. Maybe she never would.

Sally wasn't staying with us at the pub. When we'd arranged to meet up she'd looked up an old boyfriend on social media, and she'd be staying at his place for the weekend. So it was just Katie, Clara and me at The Wheatsheaf. It hadn't changed much. We used to drink in here, of course – even that summer, at fifteen. We'd get served, usually, depending who was working behind the bar. Now the place had a logo above the sign, showing that it was part of a national brewery chain, so the food would be pre-packed and the atmosphere soulless. But hey, it wasn't Janey's place. I let myself into my room and walked back into the seventies. Anaglypta wallpaper and pointless dado rails overpainted so many times it had probably reduced the volume of the room. The only interruptions to the textured walls were 'tasteful' lights with gold lampshades and tassels, and three ducks screwed to the wall. I dumped my bag on the world's saggiest bed and called home – glad for the relative sanity of Nick and the kids talking nonsense about their day.

'Are you okay, babe?' He asked in his familiar rasping voice.

'Yeah. Yes I am,' I said, clearing my throat, and banishing some of the silly ideas that had been flying around in my head.

'Sure? No, you're not. What's going on?'

'I just…' I sighed and fell back onto the bed, holding the phone to my ear. 'It's just fucking weird coming back here. I dunno.'

'It's not been that long since we were there though, has it?' It wasn't a question. He was fishing.

'Yes but when we came here before it was to see Mum and Dad. Now they're gone, it feels like I'm a stranger. But there's something else...' I restlessly turned on my side, propping myself up on an elbow.

'Go on.'

'Something's going on, and Janey kinda summoning us back here makes it feel really strange, like I've actually gone back in time or something. I almost feel like I'm fifteen again, like it's 1985.' I shivered although it wasn't cold, as if someone or something was in there with me and had run its fingers down my spine – I sat up and looked around, almost expecting to see someone in the shadows. There wasn't anyone, of course – just me.

'I'm not sure that's unusual, it's the only point of reference you've got left. It is weird, though, that email and Janey getting you back together so quickly. I know we've discussed it, but is there anything else you're not telling me? I am a bit worried. Talk to me, Flip.' Nick and I had talked at length when Janey got in touch. I don't think I'd told him about when I was a teenager – only the odd memory that cropped up in conversation. I explained about Janey, how she'd been badly burned that year. How we'd all drifted apart shortly afterwards, as if her injury had changed us all and we'd drawn a line in the sand, losing touch completely by the time we were doing our A-levels. Nick was fascinated to hear new things about my life but we did argue when I told him that I was planning to go back, that although I hadn't been in touch with the others for so long, we would all get together to see if we could help her.

So why go back? He'd said. *I wouldn't meet up with someone that I'd had no contact with for three decades, babe. You said yourself you haven't thought about the others in all that time.*

I couldn't properly explain to him why I had a sense of duty, why there was a feeling that I had to return, like the village was pulling me back. I think we all did. We never slept on an argument, but we did after this one, but the next day Nick changed some plans to cover our childcare, and didn't really ask too much more.

'It's nothing, love. Sorry, I'm just a bit tired and seeing folks after all this time is… well it's tiring.'

'How is Janey? Do you think you can help her?' I could tell from Nick's voice that he was holding back, wanting to know more, to probe and work through the whole issue. It was obviously strange for him to understand, but he knew me well enough to leave me to it. Neither of us wanted another argument and he backed down from his line of questioning.

'I think she's just stayed in this place for too long – like I told you, she hasn't even left the house. Company is going to be good for her and to talk through some things. I don't see what else we can do.'

'An intervention, as the Americans would say.'

'Yep, that's it, an intervention.'

'Okay, well as long as that's all.'

'It is and it's not. There's been something preying on my mind since we arranged this – nothing massive, nothing in the foreground, but now I'm here it's like it's always been there. Just watching.'

'Now I am officially fucking freaked out. I've never heard you talking like this.'

'It's okay, it's just like a nagging thought. Janey thinks it's this place. That it gets to you, and even when you go you never leave.'

'That's not helping.'

'I'm here because I can't remember, Nick. That summer is a façade of memories for me, and when Janey got in touch, a little of that façade peeled away. More pieces seem to be falling away all the time, and I need to find out what happened.'

'What do you mean 'what happened'?'

'To Janey, for a start.'

'You can't remember?'

'No. Honestly? No. I know she got burned somehow, and spent a shitload of time in hospital and hasn't left her house since. But there's nothing else.'

'So you weren't around when she was injured?' He was theorising now. Nick in a nutshell. 'Were you on holiday, maybe, when whatever happened, happened? That's why you can't remember, because you simply haven't got any memories of it?'

'But surely I'd remember seeing her when I came back, and visiting her in hospital and at home and all that, and I just don't. It's not just Janey, it's everything. It feels like my whole recollection is just two-dimensional and made up like a bad special effect in a film.'

'But why? How would something like that happen?'

'It feels like my memories from then don't belong to me – like I've read them somewhere – there's no depth to any of it.'

'I don't know what that means.'

'I can't explain it properly. It's like – it feels like I've suppressed something that happened, like my subconscious is hiding something from me.'

'But why would it – you – why would you do that?'

I sighed, frustrated. 'I've no idea.'

'There's nothing… bad, is there? Do I need to be as worried as I am right now?' His usually confident voice cracked.

'No, not at all. It's just closure. We'll sort Janey out, reminisce, get pissed, close it out and move on.'

'Sure?'

'Yeah,' I said unconvincingly. 'All good. Listen, I've gotta go, babe, I'm meeting the others for some horrible pub food.'

'Okay. Text me later.'

'Will do, give the boys a kiss from me.'

'Done.'

I went into the bathroom. Ignoring the mouldy silicone along the bath and the mildew on the shower curtain was one thing, but it seemed like gravity itself was different in the shower – there was so little water pressure that the water droplets barely had the energy to chuck themselves out of the end of the showerhead. It wouldn't have surprised me to see them going upwards. It was only when I was in there that I remembered how hard the water was round here, as I fought in vain to rinse the conditioner from my hair. To add insult to injury, still far from finished, the water started to run cold, so I climbed out, shivering for real this time, my body covered in goose bumps, and still with my hair full of conditioner. I was, however, determined not to let the side down and knew that Katie would be breaking out the war-paint just to make a 'remember me' statement. As I dried my hair, the degree of gnawing familiarity that I'd felt since walking into the room became clear. It was almost exactly the same as the guest house where I'd lived in my first year at university. They hadn't had enough halls of residence places to put up every fresher. The landlady had tried to be posh, and every inch the president of the local hoteliers' association. In reality she ran a fleapit. I hoped the food here was better than hers.

We'd agreed to meet in the bar at eight, and Sally had said she'd join us as well, but that was always going to depend on how 'busy' she was. I came downstairs to find Clara and Katie had got there just ahead of me. Apparently Sally would be along a little later when she'd finished 'checking in' with her fella.

'Did you call home?' Katie asked as we waited at the bar.

'Yeah, I spoke to Spock.'

'I'm sorry, who?'

'Oh yeah,' I laughed, 'I call him Spock.'

'Why,' asked Clara. 'Big ears? Flies a spaceship, maybe?'

'Because he's always so bloody logical and measured and precise in how he works things out.'

'Really? Isn't that infuriating?'

'Yes, it is, but things get done. Whilst I have to nag him – course I do – what he does is so precise that I call him Spock.'

'Wow, wish I could have such a clever nickname for mine,' grumbled Clara.

'What do you call him?' I asked.

'Smelly twat most of the time – he's always farting. I'm so glad I'm away every other month.'

'How romantic. What about you, Katie? Oh shit, sorry,' I blushed, regretting that our discussions on social media of the previous week hadn't stopped my mouth.

'No, it's okay. If he wants to fuck off with his secretary that's his look out. Here, let's grab that table.' Katie turned and busied herself paying for the drinks as we sat down. As predicted, she'd gone to town, with a fitted t-shirt and jeans, her hair half up in a clip, yet with some layers casually falling over her shoulders. It must've taken her hours. Clara and I looked positively frumpy in comparison.

'This place doesn't look like it's improved any,' Katie said, putting two glasses of gin with ice on the table we'd occupied by the window, along with three bottles of tonic.

'Do you have Fever Tree?' she'd asked when we were stood at the bar.

'We've got slimline?' said the barman, seemingly as delighted with his comprehensive assortment of mixers as he was ignorant of any others.

The glasses seemed to stick somewhat to the rustic wooden table and Katie reached for some coasters as she mouthed, *could do with a wipe.* She returned to the bar to get her vodka.

'So what do you do, Clara, I must've missed it on social media. Didn't you just say you were away every other month?' Katie asked as we finally got settled.

'Oh you wait 'til you hear this,' I said.

'I'm a geologist. I work offshore.'

'What do you mean 'offshore'?' Katie put so little tonic in her gin it wouldn't have mattered what brand it was and took a big drink.

'Oil rigs, love.'

'Bloody hell.'

'I was the first female geologist to work offshore in the UK.'

'How cool is that?' said Katie, raising her glass in a mock toast.

'It sounds a lot cooler than it actually is. I spend most of my time sitting in a control room staring at a computer screen, looking at pressure readouts from the sea bed. Feel free to think of it as cool though,' she smiled at them. 'A smelly oil rig full of beardy blokes in check shirts isn't anywhere near as cool as being a fashion designer, is it, Katie?'

'I don't really do that anymore.'

'You did Fashion at uni though, didn't you?'

'Yeah, but I couldn't really pay the rent doing it – it's so hard to break into the industry. But I met a load of designers so I ended up becoming a buyer for different fashion outlets. Because I had such a tough time, I try to support young people who are new to the industry when I can.'

'Wow, that's proper cool. Any shops I might know?' Clara seemed to recognise the irony of the question as she looked down at her entirely functional jeans and t-shirt.

'Did you ever do a range of lumberjack shirts, K?' I asked. She ignored me.

'At one point I did some buying for Debenhams, but I prefer working for smaller boutique shops – it's much more likely they'll give someone new a leg up. And as my divorce saw my bastard ex being forced to very kindly invest in my company, it's given me a little bit more financial freedom to do that.'

'So you're an 'advertising exec', right?' Clara asked, smiling as she made inverted commas with her fingers.

'That's me.'

'Anything I know? Did you do the John Lewis ad?' Katie was expectant as if everyone in advertising must've been involved with those ads at some point or another. I could specialise in advertising slug pellets for all she knew.

'No but I did Sainsbury's summer range last year.'

'Oh,' she sounded disappointed. I guess only John Lewis would do.

'Look at us,' I said with a little shake of the head, 'all growed up and moved on.'

'All except Janey, who hasn't,' said Clara, bringing us back full circle.

'She's a strange one,' Katie said. 'She always was odd, though, don't you remember? She was hanging around with us by the time we finished little school and I can't remember when that started.'

'Wasn't she always there – from the start?'

'No. Mrs Walters sat me in the front next to Clara, and Sal was next to you, Flip, in the row behind. It was always our little gang of four. Janey was there somewhere, but not at the start. Then she was just *there* and we couldn't shift her.'

'Come on, that's a bit unfair, K, we had a load of good times. She was just as much a part of the gang as the rest of us,' I said.

'She was odd, though.'

'We all were.'

'I wasn't.'

'You were odd just for hanging around with us,' said Clara.

'When I was with you guys, I could be myself and nobody was judging me.'

'It was practically like you *invented* tits, just because you grew some before anyone else. And they *did* bring all the boys to the yard!'

'Damn right.' We all smiled and Katie sat a little taller and gave her shoulders a shake to make her chest bounce. 'But it's shit when everyone calls you names. And you lot didn't.'

'You did always have a boy in tow, though, sometimes more than one.' I shrugged.

'Yeah I did, and I kissed a few guys, but I wasn't off shagging guys left-right-and-centre like people said I was.'

'Sensibilities were different then.'

"Getting off with' meant a snog, and then suddenly you were an item.'

'Not sure anyone would look twice at that now.'

'None of us really fitted in with the 'in' crowd. It's maybe why we gravitated towards each other. I don't think we were that weird though,' said Clara.

'Janey dissected birds in her spare time,' Katie wanted to illustrate her point. 'Pinned out on a chopping board. Then she pulled their guts out and put them on her wall. That's beyond 'normal' odd. I liked Spider-Man comics.'

'There *is* a difference,' Clara agreed.

'Yeah, you were a nerd,' I said.

'Fuck off!' Katie responded.

'Hey, get your own catchphrase.' Clara mimed aiming a pistol at Katie.

'So what's your point about Janey?' I asked.

'We don't hear from her in years and now we get summoned back. That's not 'normal' odd as far as I'm concerned, that's all.'

'We *have* all had dreams, King.' Clara used Katie's old nickname, 'King' Edwards. 'All the same, and all at the same time. That's gotta mean there's something more going on.'

'I'm not sure. I'm not convinced.'

'So what are you saying, that she's invented all this to bring us back here?' I asked. 'Like Friends Reunited on medication?'

'Is she on medication?' asked Clara.

'Dunno, it just came to mind.'

'Bet she is though –'

'Oh come on.' I cut Clara off with a dose of reality. 'Janey hasn't been out of her house for thirty years. She had half her body horribly burned and lost a leg – essentially saving our skins, by the way. You were expecting, perhaps, a well-adjusted, middle-aged woman with a knitting fetish?'

'I'm not middle-aged.'

'What do you mean, 'saving our skins'?' asked Katie.

'What?' I glanced at her with a frown.

'You just said about Janey getting horribly burnt by 'saving our skins'.'

'Yeah, I did, didn't I?'

'So where did you get that from?'

'I dunno.'

'You must fucking know, or you wouldn't have said it.'

'Yeah but that's the point, I *don't* know. I've got no idea how Janey got burnt.'

'So why'd you say that then?'

'I don't know, I just said, didn't I? It just came out, K. Maybe it was another piece of the façade falling away.'

'The what?'

'Nothing.'

'That's maybe what this is about, though,' said Clara.

'What do you mean?'

'Maybe it's about us coming here to revisit those bad memories, maybe it's time to deal with whatever happened. Process things.' I remembered the feeling I'd had earlier, that there'd been something – a presence – in my room.

'This is about a very lonely woman who's not had a proper conversation in thirty years and has got scared of a dream. That's why we're here.' Katie sounded sure there was nothing else in this other than Janey's fragility.

'No, it's more than that. It's about us. Even if Janey had a load of friends, I don't think she would've called anyone else, because we were there. This is about what happened that summer, remembering all we forgot.'

'There's no purpose to this, surely, Flip, it's just Janey and a dream.'

'So why did we all have the same dream when she mentioned it to us? It triggered something we've been suppressing,' said Clara.

'What'd I miss?' Sally came bounding in, looking somewhat dishevelled in t-shirt and jeans.

'A post-sex shower by the looks of you,' Katie said with a wink. Sally sat down and set a bottle of Prosecco down on the table, pouring herself a glass. 'And how was it – I mean he – I mean, oh fuck it. How are you?'

'I'm good, and he's a doll. It's almost thirty years since I last shagged him. He's a bit less spotty now.'

'A bit?' said Clara pulling a face.

'Nice.' I shared her expression.

'Well, nobody's perfect, you know.'

'We were just wondering if there was a reason behind us all coming together here, other than Janey being spooked by a dream and you wanting to get laid. Whether the dreams have done something to make us remember things. To unlock our memories.' I summarised for Sally.

'Sorry, babe, but I'm not buying any metaphysical nonsense on top of this, but even if you're right... Why?' Sally asked.

'Don't know. Maybe we've got to put all the pieces together to find out. Maybe we've got to remember everything,' I said.

'Maybe. But something bad happened that summer – and not just to those people who got burned either. Do you really wanna know it all?' There was a warning note in Clara's voice.

'Don't you?' I asked.

'Sorry, how do we know that bad things happened?' Sally asked and took a long drink from her glass. We all chipped in to describe the events of the afternoon at Janey's – the dreams, the Shadow Man and Ethel Grimshaw. 'We don't know for sure that more bad things happened.' Sally took a long drink from her glass.

'We know people died.'

'Well, one person.'

'Yeah, but how many more?' asked Clara.

'And what has any of this got to do with us? Maybe it was all a coincidence?' asked Sally.

'There're a lot of missing pieces, Sal,' I replied. 'One person burned to death and I don't know how, but I've got a feeling there were others that we haven't remembered yet. And none of us can remember what happened to Janey.'

'Do I want to find out that something terrible happened to us, to Janey, that *we* might have done something equally terrible? Some things are better left forgotten.' Clara shrugged.

'I'd just as soon be at home, having had a barbecue and planning to go and watch my son play cricket tomorrow, but now we're here, I think some closure would be good,' I reasoned.

'So you're not pleased to see us?' Sally asked with mock offence.

'Somebody was,' snorted Clara.

'De-fucking-lighted, darling. No, it is nice to see you, but that isn't what this is about,' I said.

'So what's happened to Janey?' Sally asked.

'Nothing's happened to her, that's the problem,' Katie replied.

'No, this place has,' Clara was clearly working up to something.

'You're starting to sound like Janey now,' I said.

'What do you mean? You're not suggesting this place is evil and getting all spooky-majooky on us again are you?'

'No, K, I'm not. But if she'd got out of here, gone to university, got herself a decent leg, been trained to walk again and had some plastic surgery, she could've met someone and been living with her two kids in Whitstable or somewhere. She could be a school governor or something.' Clara shrugged.

'Maybe she doesn't want plastic surgery, maybe she's happy how she is,' I said.

'Oh fuck off. You've seen her, she has to be careful that her eye doesn't fall out of its socket when she looks down. She's as trapped here as she is in that body.' Clara looked at each of us, and we all knew it was true.

'This place is the back of beyond. It's run down, it doesn't offer anything. It's like admitting defeat, living here,' Sally added.

'So it's draining her, she's got no... got no *hwyl*, as the Welsh say,' I said.

'What the hell is *that*?' Katie asked, her immaculately plucked eyebrows raised.

'It's like your energy, King, your life, your drive. When someone gives up, they've lost their hwyl.'

'Nice.'

'That's just it then, she's a bit flat 'cos this place is a shit hole? And because of that she's having dreams, or inventing dreams that we then somehow have too? How the hell is that happening?' Katie asked.

'If you're not buying the story, what do you think it is? Is she imagining things? Because if she is, how are we imagining the same thing too? Group hallucination or delusion?' Sally pressed.

'*Do* we think she's just imagining things?' Clara asked.

'The dreams?'

'Yeah.' Clara nodded

'I don't know what she thinks is out there,' Sally said with a shrug.

'Very Fox Mulder.'

'The Shadow Man,' Katie said it because someone needed to.

'Yeah but what is it? To her it's an idea, a concept, a *thing*. But what is it really? A monster? A religious cult that burns people? Aliens? What?' Sally was being quite aggressive.

'Hang on now girls, let's take a step back, there's no need to get in each other's face.' Like always, I was the moderator.

'Yeah, okay. Sorry. I'm talking through the prosecco filter.' Sally gave a cheeky *what do you know* shrug and finished her second glass.

'Okay. I'm sorry too.' Katie playfully punched Sally on the shoulder.

'But let's think. We've all forgotten things from when we were teenagers. I'd forgotten you fell through the ice, Flip, but Katie and I were chatting about it earlier and she'd remembered,' Clara said. 'You see, we forget things, but others remember, and two people might remember the same thing in different ways. When you fell through the ice, Katie thought it was funny, but you thought you were gonna die. That's the point. We don't all forget the same thing, or groups of things. As far as I can make out – and I haven't done masses of research, but I did some – the only way that people forget whole periods of time is when they don't want to remember, when the thought of remembering is too traumatic. So what the fuck happened that made us all deliberately forget it for thirty years? Just what could have been so fucking horrible?'

Chapter 5

— Then —

The Lake

We cycled from Janey's to the end of Stow Lane and turned onto Lake Road, an old lane running by the park entrance then out into the countryside. The tarmac meandered lazily along the verge like it had spread up to the edge of the grass rather than the other way around. Crisp modern bungalows, built just ten years before, sat awkwardly amongst ancient weeping willow, sycamore and oak, their large gardens and 'modern' planting of eucalyptus and palm trees destined to merge with the old over time. Middle-aged people worked in their front gardens, separated from the verge by low walls of the same yellow brick as their homes. Occasionally a tractor would roar past like a giant green dragon with a mysterious tail of tines and blades and murderous intent. Aside from that, the road was so quiet that the residents treated the verge as an extension of their gardens, lovingly tending the grass and even planting shrubs and bulbs.

We cycled slowly, snaking wildly across the road, talking about nothing in particular, five-abreast in the knowledge we'd hear cars before seeing them. On that hot summer day even the breeze was warm, offering no respite from the heat as we passed the old signpost denoting that we were leaving the village. Hedgerows replaced gardens, large swathes of brambles clothed the hawthorn hedges with swarms of butterflies in attendance, and the breeze was thick with pollen. Huge patches of nettles stood guard just off the verge, waiting with a world of pain for the wayward cyclist.

I heard the distinctive 'peewit' call of lapwings as they drifted and tumbled on the wind that blew across the wheat fields and bustled around the trees and bushes, sounding almost like the sea gently rising and falling on the shore at Bridlington on a summer day out.

'I'm sweating like a pig,' said Katie, taking one hand off the handlebars and wafting the bottom of her 'Wake Me Up Before You Go-Go' t-shirt to create some airflow.

'Look out, look out, she's getting 'em out!' shouted Clara, then, pleased with her rhyme, she said it over and over again until everyone joined in. 'Look out, look out, she's getting 'em out! Look out, look out, she's getting 'em out!'

'Alright you lot, you can all –'

'She can't be though, Chris Whiteman isn't here,' Clara corrected herself.

'Yeah, she'd get 'em out for Chris, alright,' Janey said.

'Shut up you lot!'

'You did though, didn't you?' I joined in.

'No! Someone caught us and he had his hand inside my top.'

'And that's sooooo different because..?' Janey heard the noise of a car engine as we approached a sharp right-hand bend ahead. 'Car!'

The car appeared ahead of us like liquid, shimmering in the heat haze above the tarmac. It was travelling at speed, wheels on the edge of screeching as it hugged the bend, seeming to lose traction before the rubber regained purchase and drove the car straight toward us.

'Sh–' said Clara, wobbling precariously after she'd drifted almost to the other side of the road. The rest of us tucked into single file on the left, but she was stranded and neither car nor bike had anywhere to go. Clara aimed for the open gateway of a field, pushing down hard on the pedals, overcoming inertia to increase her speed. Her front wheel left the tarmac and hit the edge of a large wheel rut, hard-baked mud behaving more like concrete, stopping the tyre dead, flipping bike and rider into the air. She executed an almost perfect flip over the handlebars, landing in a sitting position – a pile of fresh, ripe cowshit breaking her fall.

'Oh fuck off!' Clara said, slapping her hands angrily on the ground. 'Fucking road hog!' she shouted to the driver of the car who'd slowed almost to a stop, Van Halen's *Jump* blaring through the open windows of the car. I could only see the silhouette of the young driver and didn't recognise the car. He gunned the engine and tooted the horn repeatedly as he roared off down the road.

Clara found a patch of dock leaves and used them in a vain attempt to clean herself up, but only succeeded in smearing the slimy green shit more uniformly over her stonewashed denim cut-offs. Eventually she gave up as she realised it was only going to come off with Persil and a power wash. We started cycling down the road again, Clara taking the lead, the rest of us following close behind, making moo-ing sounds, or asking each other in exaggerated stage-whispers if they could *detect a funny smell?*

'Fuck. Off.' Clara turned to fire off an angry expletive. We kept repeating ourselves and she kept repeating the same response.

'Fuck off.'

'Fuck off.'

'Fuck off.' We found this and her reaction so funny that it became her catchphrase – swearing did seem to come naturally to Clara.

After another mile we passed the giant modern mansion on the left, complete with ostentatious lion statues on the gateposts, and the Parthenon-esque pillars of the front porch. Someone had said that the guy who owned the house was an ex-footballer who'd ended up in prison for handling money from gangsters, and that's how they could afford such a big house. We'd never hear of money laundering back then, and I remember asking my dad about it whilst having this image of someone washing huge bags of money in the launderette and then tumbling it in one of those big dryers.

We'd left the village far behind and the wide-open farmland stretched away to our left, falling gently away on a slope from our slightly raised view, fields of wheat, corn and rapeseed filled the land. The hedges on the right were replaced by thick woodland – decidedly different but just as dense and impenetrable. Hidden away in here was the narrow track leading to the first lake. Further on up the road was a right turn onto a 'Y'-shaped farm track, deeply rutted from heavy farm vehicles during the wet winter.

'Good job there's no shit for you to land in here, Clara!' I said, wobbling off the edge of a rut, having some sympathy for the tumble she had taken. It was almost impossible to ride along the track, and after several falls we decided to push our bikes. The lane forked, curving slowly away to the right and the second lake, with the left-hand fork turning sharply up toward farm buildings. A large sign guarded the fork stating *Keep Out – Newlands Farm and Quarry – Private Property.* The farmer never liked people coming on to his land, and the sign deterred dog walkers and other kids from the village, but it was actually a public right-of-way, meaning he could do nothing but grumble when we did. We always enjoyed seeing him outside in the yard as we passed by, giving him a cheery wave as he glared back at us, disapprovingly, no doubt wondering where we were going. Or maybe he always knew. It wasn't rocket science.

∞ ∞ ∞

The lake. We'd been cycling up here for years, since we were eleven and first allowed to roam round the local villages on our bikes by ourselves. It was different back then. Mum and Dad would never know where I was from about ten in the morning until six at night when I'd have to be home. Sometimes I'd pop back for lunch, sometimes there were a few of us, sometimes we'd land on someone else's doorstep. It all seemed to work and everything was safe. Now, with my kids, I need to know where they're going, how long they're going to be there, to text if they're going somewhere else, and I certainly need to know that they aren't just marauding around on their bikes in the leafy villages of our home in Shropshire.

We didn't just go there in the summer, though. We'd crash through the dead undergrowth in the autumn and winter, weaving our way between the naked trees, disturbing pheasants and partridge hiding from the local shoot, to stand at the edge of the inky-black water, watching gentle ripples disturb the mirror-like surface.

Early one bitingly cold Saturday morning the previous winter, we'd decided to get out and see the frost-scape for ourselves. A week of clear skies and watery sunshine had meant that temperatures had plummeted and we'd gathered at the edge of the park in Parka jackets, Aran jumpers and wellington boots. It was too cold to cycle quickly, taking in the hedgerows that looked like they'd been covered in icing along Lake Road, which was white with road salt instead of frost, but at least it wasn't slippery. Trees and bushes, denuded of leaves, were brilliant white or silver, the surrounding soil similarly iced over like we'd been transported into some winter wonderland Christmas card, and all we needed now was some jolly fat bloke to come 'Ho-ho-ho-ing' across the scene.

We turned up the track to Newlands and didn't even try to cycle. Where the verges and brambles had died back, branches and twigs stuck upright from the frozen ground like strange alien hands and fingers. The landscape was almost unrecognisable, as if we hadn't been here before, the stillness and silence eerie in such a familiar place. Our footsteps were muffled by the frozen grass yet amplified across the fields to scare gamebirds into flight. Emerging by the lake gave us some welcome familiarity. The moorhens and geese had gone for the winter and so all was silent here as well. The softly curving bank that we called our 'beach', usually so private with its dense backdrop of foliage, was exposed and open, the skeletons behind unable to hide anything in their nakedness.

We walked to the edge of the bank where bulrushes were immobilised in the frozen water. Jack Frost had arrived so quickly that he'd even captured the ripples on the lake with his icy fingers. We busied ourselves throwing stones onto the frozen surface, to see if we could make it crack. Fairly quickly deciding that small stones weren't good enough, we searched for bigger and more impressive rocks to use, culminating in one huge specimen that took both Katie and Janey to heave into the air and onto the ice shelf.

It held firm.

Pushing aside the frozen grass and bulrushes, I tentatively stepped out onto the ice.

'What are you doing?' Katie asked.

'Going for a skate. Anyone wanna join me?' I slid out unsteadily onto the surface in my wellies, staying close to the water's edge, confident the ice was thick enough but not brave enough to venture further out. I skidded across the surface, doing my best Torvill and Dean impression, my boots being far more at home wading through mud and cow shit than trekking on the Laurendon glacier. My confidence grew and I slithered further out onto the lake, the rippled surface the only thing to slow me down. I couldn't see water flowing up onto the ice anywhere, nor was there any open water in the distance, so I was confident it would hold, but I wasn't prepared to go out to the middle – that would've been like setting out for the North Pole – and I was already so far out of my comfort zone that I went a little nearer the bank.

'Come on,' I said, waving my arms at the others. I jumped up and down a couple of times on the ice to show them how safe and thick it was. 'See, it's fine.' Sally and Clara pushed through the frozen grasses at the edge to take a step onto the ice, but didn't come any further. I repeated my jump, several times. 'Come on, guys!' Enjoying the slight splashing sound I was making, but not thinking any more of it. The others still needed some convincing, so I decided to try once more, jumping in the air and landing hard, I heard an almighty crack from somewhere behind me and the sound of water rushing. I'd already programmed my muscles to take off again and the First Duke of Wellington's finest propelled me skywards once more, even as I saw the ice open in a yawning gap beneath my feet.

'Oh shit,' was all I could muster before I landed on ice that was now no more than a wafer, and went straight through with almost no resistance. Blind panic hit me as I sank. In that moment I didn't know how far out I was, or how deep the water beneath me would be. Instinctively I spread my arms wide to stop myself going straight under the frozen surface, otherwise that could've been it. The biting cold gripped my torso like a vice, squeezing all the breath from my body. My legs went numb instantly as I tried to kick to propel me out and onto the ice again. I looked to the shore for help where Katie and Janey were pissing themselves laughing, but Clara and Sally realised straight away that I was actually in a lot of trouble. They carefully 'bambied' out to my rescue, swearing and shouting at each other that they were on thinner ice and that they were going to go in like me. Finally they got close enough for Clara to lay on her front and reach out a hand to me, and for Sally to pull her legs and yank us both out. Before long I was back on terra firma, with Katie and Janey still laughing as I shivered uncontrollably. The three-mile cycle home was the longest I'd ever known. My drainpipe jeans squeezing ever tighter, giving no protection from the icy breeze that had got up on that cold, crisp day. My heavy wool jumper dragging me down as it dripped a trail along the road. I got in and dashed upstairs, avoiding my parents, so I could get quickly out of my soaking wet clothes and stash the evidence. I didn't want to explain to them what had happened. Dad would've lost it, and that would be that for my visits to the lake. I ended up sitting in a bath of lukewarm water, which was all my chilblains would tolerate.

∞ ∞ ∞

Mis-adventure aside, the lake was our place. Of seclusion and escape, from our parents, from homework, from daily chores, from bullies and other idiots, from Clara's older brother. It was freedom. Actually, Clara's older brother did have his uses, like my brother Ray, when they used to sneak us alcohol from the shop so we could get a bit pissed prior to the cycle home.

∞ ∞ ∞

The hard-baked farm lane stretched away in front of us, meandering to the right then left. The shimmering heat haze creating a blurred curtain in the distance, the dusty track a sharp contrast to the green of the maize growing in the fields. A large irrigation system was at work – like every summer, it seemed – with huge hose reels attached to a water cannon that slowly rotated around a pre-defined arc, or a weird-looking trailer with a huge bar extending either side, watering a strip of land as it slowly moved along. The rhythmical spurt of a water jet some distance away was the only sound to disrupt the birdsong as we walked along.

'Oh, I need a pee,' said Sally.

'You always need to pee, you're as bad as my dad – but he's bloody old,' Katie replied.

'It's the sound of that sprinkler thing, making me want to go.'

'Bloody hell. Won't be long now love and you can make a nice patch of warm water in the lake.'

'Euw, do you mind, I've gotta swim in that,' said Clara.

'What, you've never pissed in the lake?'

'No. Have you?' Clara looked at each of us, seeing the same *when in Rome* expressions.

'The lake is full of duck shit, Clara, seriously. What are you worried about?' said Katie.

'Oh fuck off, you lot are disgusting.' The path rose to a small bridge across a wide dry ditch, then through a copse of huge oak trees – there were a few of these on this stretch of farmland. We were getting close now. The maize field was still on our right, but there was no more farmland after the trees to our left. A wide patch of nettles and scrub had been left alone, surrounding the rusting skeleton of an old collapsed barn, the frame itself the only remnant, and that looked like it was on borrowed time. At the far side was the squat hulk of a long dead farm machine – a baler perhaps or some other such device, now sitting quietly watching like a giant toad. It was impossible to tell its original colour as it was now a rusted red-brown, with holes where the panelling had given up the ghost. Some lettering remained – it might have been made by New Holland if you pieced them together and used your imagination. The track sloped gently upwards now, and a grassy bank appeared on our left rising above the nettles that were the baler jailers. The track itself curved away to the right around the densely planted wood that sheltered the northern side of the lake, and continued on to the top lake.

I always loved the moment when we walked up that slope and caught our first glimpse of the water, the sun glinting, the gentle ripples disrupting the mirror surface. Clumps of reeds and bullrushes grew out of the margins to form a foliage barrier. Other parts of the bank sloped gently down to the water to create a bog – guaranteed to suck the unwary up to their knees and necessitate panicked crying, much laughter, really terrible language, the temptation to leave them where they were, followed ultimately by human versus mud tug-of-war to get them out.

Our bikes discarded in their usual place on the edge of the track as it curved away, we hiked around the edge of the water to reach the trees. The lake was kidney shaped and about half a mile in length. Our spot was about a third of the way along, as the bank started to curve back in to the water again. There was a shallow lagoon – a shelf left by the giant quarrying machines of years ago no doubt – before the water went much deeper and colder out in the middle. I had heard of some diving clubs using the lake for practising but we'd never seen any evidence of them. Maybe they were exceptionally good divers and that's why we hadn't seen them? The ground rose gently away from the lagoon, and rose to a curved bank in front of the dense foliage of the treeline.

Our beach.

The bank curved round toward the waterline and extended out into the water, making the kidney-shape of the lake. Bushes crowded onto this small peninsula and a lone tree stood at the point, reaching up and out over the deeper water. Dragonflies buzzed across the surface searching for tiny insects, then stopped to hover above the reeds. They were incredibly coloured in red or blue, and their wings glinted as they skimmed the water. We dropped our bags by the treeline, unfurling our towels like tourists on sun loungers in the Costa Brava. We stashed our snacks and drinks under the shade of the trees then got ready to get wet. The first few times we'd been swimming at the lake we'd taken costumes, but then one of us – I think it was Katie – had forgotten theirs and just went skinny-dipping. After that nobody wore a costume.

'Our lagoon awaits, ladies,' I said, not at all self-conscious about my body anymore. I wasn't a Katie, but my body was developing. I now seemed to attract the attention of the boys at school, which was nice I suppose, but then again, almost all of them were total idiots. We stepped into the water. Shallow lagoon or not, in a baking hot summer, that first step was always bloody cold – an immediate icy chill grabbing your toes. You never withdrew though – once you were committed that was it. Shriek as much as you like, of course, the prerogative of the teenage girl, but never pull back. Nobody ever leapt straight into the deep part off the point by the tree, not until they'd properly 'got in' and become acclimatised to the water. We'd spend time bobbing around until it felt really warm before we'd jump off there. Sometimes we'd swim from the lagoon, round the point and feel the sudden change in temperature as the shelf disappeared beneath us. I always envisaged a huge lake monster swimming beneath us, or a freshwater shark coming up from the depths. The shivering wasn't just the cold. Clara or Katie would be first to the tree, and to unwrap the rope that we'd hung from the large overhanging branch – Janey had climbed the tree at the start of the summer to tie the rope as far along the branch as she dared, but she'd overbalanced and turned a somersault before face-planting in the water. With a shriek and a scream as each of us hit the cold surface, the silly stunts and nonsense would begin.

When we were borderline hypothermic, and shivering from genuine cold rather than irrational fear, we would flop down on our towels to work on our suntans. Back then no one used sun cream, that was only something you used on holiday – 'you never burn at home,' Mum said. It was something to do with sea air, apparently. I wasn't too familiar with the chemistry and physics of ultraviolet absorption through a salt layer, but Mum was obviously an expert. When we did go on holiday, she always bought the sun cream with a '2' on the tube. Any bigger numbers were irrelevant, and more expensive. Of course, when we still burned to a crisp after spending all day in the sun, she would always explain 'that I *did* put sun cream on', because factor two Ambre Solaire would act as a complete block on the surface of the sun itself. Somehow we'd managed to work a system of gradual exposure at the lake, interspersed by regular dips, and whilst we'd always look a bit pink around the gills at the end of the day, we rarely did burn badly, and always had incredible tans by the time school started again after the summer.

As we lay dozing in the sun, I remember thinking about a scary Public Information Film that they used to show between adverts on the TV. It had shown kids playing by open water, being watched over by a hooded figure that was obviously Death. As irrational as the fear of the freshwater shark, I would always look around to make sure the grim reaper was elsewhere that day. And not hiding in the trees. There were no monsters – not really – and nothing bad was *really* going to happen at our lake.

Chapter 6

— Now —

The Idyllic Village

A watched pot never boils.

Well, Janey's kettle certainly never seemed to as we stood over it, desperate for another cup of coffee to push back the hangover. I'm almost fifty with two kids, a husband and a responsible job. I don't really expect an evening discussing the strange events of a summer thirty years ago to degenerate into drinking competitions and talking about shagging.

But it had.

The idea of the 'full grease' for breakfast, served in the same room — at the same table in fact — where I'd got so drunk didn't appeal, so I soaked up last night's gin and prosecco with three triangles of toast. The others seemed to be faring better than me, although we could all do with a cuppa to get us going. As the kettle didn't boil, we milled around between the small kitchen and only slightly bigger 'middle' room. I never could fathom middle rooms – linking a kitchen to somewhere else, a hallway in this case, they were never big enough to do anything with but took up too much space to completely waste. Janey had an ancient green Dralon sofa in hers, where only patches of the velour remained and, like the suite in the lounge, some of the foam underneath poked out. Janey was clucking around, trying to keep everyone happy. She looked better than yesterday, and I wondered if she'd been nervous – either about seeing us for the first time in decades or just interacting with other humans. It was quite comical, the way she was taking everyone's exact tea and coffee orders.

'Janey, what's in the black greenhouse, m'darlin'?' Katie was looking out of the side kitchen window.

'It's a polytunnel. I had it fixed to the back of the house so the back door opens into it – means I don't have to go outside. It's great to grow your own stuff.' We could see the curved tunnel sticking out into the garden, thick black polythene stretched across the whole frame. The rest of the garden was a wasteland. Waist-high grass sticking up in tufts or fallen over under its own weight in the morning dew. Huge patches of brambles and nettles grew where there'd been borders and vegetables when we were kids. It looked just as one would've expected of a garden that'd gone feral for thirty years.

'What, like tomatoes and cucumbers and stuff?' Clara asked as she filled some mugs with the now finally boiling water.

'No,' she did her half smile that no one could get used to. 'They'd never grow in something blacked-out like that, would they? It's a mushroom farm – you need a special growing area where you control the light, temperature and humidity, so I had mine blacked out. Quite a few growers do that.'

'Get through a lot of mushrooms, do you?' asked Sally, between sips of Yorkshire tea. Everyone else smiled.

'Not just your regular mushrooms. I grow *Psilocybe cubensis.*'

'Course you do, and you've become Alan fucking Titchmarsh while we've been away. You think you know someone. What are they?' Clara looked at Janey over the top of her mug.

'Magic mushrooms.'

'Fuck off!'

'Just like the ones we used to find down by the lake.'

'You're not selling them online to make a living, are you?' I asked, only half joking, still wondering what she did with her time.

'No,' Janey smirked. 'I use them for pain relief for my leg.'

'Oh,' I replied, and the jovial mood suddenly changed as we all exchanged a glance, thankfully missed by Janey, as she continued to fuss around us. It wasn't that I'd put my foot in it, it was just the size of the shoe. 'I've been in pain since the accident and the doctors have been bloody useless. I went to pain clinics and acupuncturists – Mum and Dad insisted on trying to take me to anyone that might help.' I noted that she sounded almost critical of her parents for doing so.

'I'd do the same for my kids.' was all I could respond with.

'Looking like I did. Like I do. And walking with a limp, I guess I started to withdraw from everywhere – from everyone. So the last thing I wanted was people fussing around me. I think I musta been so rude to some of those people – there were quite a lot that we only ever went to once.'

'Did you ever find any treatment that did seem to work, or to be worthwhile sticking with?' I was never one to avoid the difficult questions.

'It was getting harder and harder for me to leave the house, and I think I got so worked up that any benefit my treatment might have had was completely eclipsed. So, no, I guess is the answer to your question. In the end I did a lot of research and looked into how people were using cannabis for pain relief. But it's not that easy to get hold of it when you don't leave the house.'

'Amazon not sell it then?' asked Katie, enjoying the conversation.

'Not yet, but it'll only be a matter of time. I did manage to get some in the end from some people I knew online.' I thought later that her comment sounded a little weird. *Some people I knew online.* Not *friends*, not people that she met in a chatroom and got friendly with on Facebook, just some people she became acquainted with. As if Uber provided a drug-dealing service. 'But it didn't really work, and I didn't like smoking it or putting it in food. It was weird, it just never seemed to do anything for me.'

'So you can buy magic mushrooms online?' Clara asked – too aghast this time even for an expletive.

'No,' laughed Janey. 'Well, not quite how you think. You buy spores, and you can source them online, yes. I'm not sure how desperately legal it is, and you need to do quite a lot with those spores to produce the mushrooms. They aren't easy buggers to grow. But yes, they are freely available on the web.'

'So that's how you source yours?'

'It is now, but I didn't start like that.'

'Now you're going to have to explain yourself. Blimey, you think you know someone!' Katie exclaimed, echoing Clara's earlier comment.

'It was on the day of Mum and Dad's funeral.'

'Oh God, I'm sorry;'

'It's okay, Katie, really. The worst part about the day was having to go outside. I smoked some pot and then got shitfaced. People just thought it was the grief, and I didn't really speak to anyone. I had to get out of there, and someone took me out to the lake – I don't even remember who, a cousin I think. I sat on the bank and looked across the grass leading to the old nettle patch and the barn, and I saw mushrooms growing. The same ones we used back then.'

'I remember being off my tits on more than one occasion, when it definitely wasn't just your mum's vodka,' said Clara.

'Yes, we did get through some 'tea' back then. So there they were, and I dug them up and put them in the back of my cousin's car to bring home. I totally forgot about the wake and the rest of my family. I ordered the polytunnel and managed to get a crop from the first batch I grew. When I exhausted that culture, I had to look to the web because I've not been outside again since.'

'And they work?'

'I'm sorry, Clara?'

'They help you with your pain?'

'Oh yeah, definitely.'

'Can I see inside your polytunnel?' Katie asked.

'Well, yeah, I s'pose. But it's just like a dark room with some damp soil in it. There's not even any mushrooms growing in it at the moment - I'm all out.'

'So how're you managing for pain relief?' I asked.

'Oh, I dry most of my stock then freeze them, so I've always got a certain amount. You don't just take it willy-nilly, you dose it out like medication. Otherwise *I* would be off my tits half the time.' There was a pause – it seemed that the subject was exhausted and nobody had any more questions for Janey. 'Anybody dream last night?' she asked.

'Sorry, too pissed,' I said.

'I did,' said Katie. 'It was horrible, actually. I was in my room, in bed, asleep. Then I woke up, like, with a start. It was dark and cold, and getting colder and I just knew something was in there with me – someone. I was gonna scream when suddenly he was on top of me – this dark figure – he was just a dark weight in a cloak or something, and he put his hands round my throat and started choking me. I couldn't make a sound, his thumbs were crushing my windpipe and his face got closer and closer to mine before I passed out. Then I woke up.'

'Fuck me,' said Clara.

'Shit, that's bloody awful, King, are you okay?'

'Well I am now, Flip, no problem. But I almost shat the bed last night.'

We all took a break to use the bathroom and help make more tea and coffee. It was wearing having to try and remember so much, and to weave these new memories in with the old – working out what to discard because it was too plastic, or linear, or poorly realised. We had to kick the B-movie out of our memories.

'Janes, yesterday you mentioned the Shadow Man. I remember the name now, and some of how he scared us. Do you remember how he came about – where we conjured him from? Was he real?'

'We didn't conjure him, Flip, he's real.'

'Really?' asked Katie, disbelievingly.

'Does anyone remember me reading those magazines that summer – *The Unexplained*?'

'Didn't you show some of them to us?'

'Yeah, they had articles about Nessie and Bigfoot and all that stuff.'

'Oh yeah – they had spontaneous combustion pics – I remember now. You got out this well-thumbed magazine and showed us some dodgy pictures – it was like a nerd porno,' said Clara.

'Thanks.'

'I didn't really mean about the nerd bit.'

'Yeah you did – we were nerds. That's why the dicks largely left us alone. Largely.' I wasn't sure but had an inkling about what Janey meant – like there was a memory about to return.

'There was an article in one about spirits and bogeymen, so I went searching for books on the subject in the library. Unsurprisingly there wasn't a lot of choice, but I found one, can't remember the author's name, but it was all about odd cases in the North of England – unexplained deaths and disappearances, that kind of thing. There wasn't much on it, but there was a short article about The Shadow Man of North Lincolnshire.'

'And who was he?' I asked.

'It was like, late seventeen hundreds, and Laurendon was a decent-sized village even then – mainly from wealthy landowners bringing in workers to live and work in the fields. The hill was a natural border between three estates and they couldn't easily farm on it, so they built farm cottages and buildings on the slopes and it meant the workers were quite central. It'd been happening for hundreds of years, so the village just grew and there was a shop and an inn. Then kids started going missing, people got burned inexplicably and they decided that it was someone who lurked in the shadows before pouncing on their victims. They decided it was this one guy who'd done it.'

'Did they have any evidence or proof?'

'You have to remember this was way back then. There wasn't a police force. It was like a mob that went around accusing anyone and everyone and you really had to prove you didn't do it. They found this guy, a bit of a misfit, a loner, and the story is that they found scraps of the kids' clothing in his house, and decided that made him guilty.'

'And what happened?'

'They burned him at the stake on the island in the pond.'

'In the middle of the village?'

'Yep.'

'Shit, yes I remember now – that's definitely not the first time I've heard that,' the memory exploded in my head like a firework.

'And there are recorded events – burnings, kids going missing periodically ever since. And now with this story in the paper about someone else getting burned, it feels like the whole thing is starting again.'

'So how can that be – people going missing over the years and even now?' I asked.

'It's gotta be a copycat,' said Katie as if she were stopping any debate before it started.

'What, every couple of decades someone else will fancy their chances of being The Shadow Man?' Janey shook her head. 'It's not like someone else having a go at being Bruce Wayne.'

'So what then? It can't be him, he's dead.'

'It's this place. It gets to you. It's like his spirit or whatever is possessing the village.'

'Janey, are you aware of how fucked up and crazy that sounds?'

'Acutely.'

'I'm not so sure I completely disagree with Janey on this one,' I said.

'What?' said Clara.

'Thanks for the support – I think,' Janey shrugged and sat down to take the weight off her leg.

'I think the veneer of this place peeled away when I left.'

'What does *that* mean?' asked Sal.

'I mean it isn't how it seemed to me when I lived here, and I can now see it for what it is.'

'So when you used to come back to see your folks, what did it feel like to you?' Katie asked.

'I think after uni… Well, while I was at uni it wasn't much different – apart from being able to get served in pubs and stuff. So I'd come home and hook up with whoever was around, get pissed and not really talk about the place.'

'Yet we never got together when we came home. The only people we really knew, we seemed to have forgotten,' said Sal.

'What about after, Flip?' Katie continued.

'It was like the string was cut. Like there wasn't a link any more. I'd come home a few times a year and Mum and Dad would come down to us about the same. Spock always made a point of inviting them and welcoming them – they were good to us.'

'Did you all get along?'

'We did and we didn't – it wasn't that, we just weren't close. It was like they were entrenched *here,* and the bullshit and sensibilities of here and how *here* thought you should be. But they helped us out a lot and we wanted to show our gratitude by making them welcome, and it kinda worked.'

'Kind of?'

'We were glad when they went home, right enough.' I couldn't stifle a smile.

'And when you say the string was cut, was that with the village as well?' Clara asked.

'I think it just faded. It just became anywhere-ville. I always think of it as my home village but it's not, it's just a canvas on which I painted my childhood.'

'Christ that's deep,' nodded Clara in appreciation.

'So you don't feel any affinity to the place now?' Katie almost looked like she was hurt by what I was saying.

'No. In all honesty, not at all. There were memories of that summer, particularly, that were vivid for me, snippets of us at the lake and riding round that were some of my most treasured memories. But that was before this weekend. Now we're finding out what really happened it's like every good memory is fading, like the lights are being switched off and the village is fading into the darkness.'

'Bloody hell, Flip.'

'So what do you think of the place?' Janey pushed, wanting more from me.

'Grubby. It's like something's going on beneath the surface and we're scratching at it and what's underneath is... grubby.'

'This place has a dark heart,' said Janey, nodding in agreement. 'It sucks the life out of you. Maybe it's the Shadow Man and he lives off it.'

'You're talking souls and all that, right?' asked Sal, wide-eyed.

'Yeah, maybe. We've already talked about the people that died, businesses die too, they get set up and flounder around for a couple of years then disappear—'

'But it's a little village out in the sticks, and quite a way from bigger towns. I think that's normal, isn't it?'

'Bullshit,' Janey spat. 'You look at the number of executive houses that've been built in the last twenty years for outsiders moving in. People with money. A commute to any one of six or seven towns or cities is under an hour so you can live in the country and work in the city. Perfect. The place should be flourishing. Yet it isn't. And people are dying. It's like the place destroys you.'

'Oh, fuck off, guys.'

Chapter 7

— Then —

Todd Ainsworth

If nothing bad could happen at our lake, it followed that nothing bad could happen in our village. How could it? Bad things happened in other places.

And then Mrs Grimshaw burned to death, so that was that idea out of the window. Surely that was it, right?

But then Todd Ainsworth died.

Todd was a few years older than us, and a bit of a loner. No, he was worse than that, he was downright odd. He'd drive past in his sky-blue Ford Capri and make all kinds of lurid and suggestive comments to us. He was creepy. Todd had been in the bottom set for everything at school and might well have been diagnosed with some form of developmental disorder these days, but back then he was just thick and weird. Not the brightest star in the sky, Todd wasn't the prettiest either. He had a high forehead and his eyes weren't level, one was higher than the other – like he'd had his head squeezed in a vice or something. His thin face was all goofy with teeth – like Plug from the *Beano* – and a lopsided mouth. He was every orthodontist's nightmare.

He left school with nothing and his dad had almost been forced into training him to be a mechanic in the family garage – there was nothing else for him to do other than sitting at home in his pants watching daytime TV, which was just becoming a thing. Now, it seemed, when he wasn't playing with himself, he was playing with cars. Todd had always been a pest. He'd got a car, and so, freakish as he was, there were some girls in our year who were bizarrely drawn to him. That meant, of course, in his vice-squashed mind, that he was God's gift to women, and every single one of us would swoon in front of him. He'd drive round the village stalking us as we rode around, passing us rather too frequently for our liking, making a nuisance of himself. He'd call us his *birds*, and I think he genuinely believed we'd all succumb to his masculine charms, probably in sequence.

Like a lot of things, stalking hadn't been invented back then, but that's definitely what he did to us. This seemed to increase after Mrs Grimshaw died – we didn't seem to be able to go anywhere without his car appearing and following us. Maybe he thought that the notoriety of the village made him even more irresistible, or maybe one shouldn't read too much into the mess inside his head. Sometimes he'd follow us at a distance, coasting along, shadowing us a few hundred yards behind no matter where we went. Stopping when we did, crawling along when we set off. It was like the spooky goings on had brought the weirdos out.

That day he caught up with us on Coopers Lane, pulling up alongside as we rode around the pond, ducks and Canada geese scattering as he sounded his ridiculous two-tone horn – it had only been cool on *The Dukes of Hazzard*.

'Where you going, girls?' he asked.

'Nowhere exciting, Todd.' Katie would extend the vowel sound in his name so it sounded like 'Toad'. Despite being three or four years older than we were, he still couldn't grow anything more than facial fuzz, no matter how hard he tried. He'd grown his hair too, but it was thin and patchy, so he looked like a middle-aged hippie trying to be cool.

'Any of you fancy coming for a ride in my car?' His crooked, toothy smile was like a leer even when he wasn't being suggestive. 'We can have a ride in more ways than one if you'd like.' And then the leer widened and became quite frightening.

'Oh fuck off, Todd!' I talked too much – verbal diarrhoea, Mum called it – and I knew it pissed some people off, but I just couldn't stop myself. I was, however, the least sweary of the group – at least I had a filter for that – closely followed by Janey and Sally, and a long way behind Clara and Katie. But not when it came to Todd, who always seemed to push my buttons.

'That's a really pretty mouth you've got, Flip. I could use a mouth like that.'

'Oh you're fucking gross, just fuck off and leave us alone, you creep.' Clara had clearly had enough of him as well.

'Oh okay,' he nodded with feigned disappointment. 'Not even for a toke on this?' He leered again as he raised a freshly rolled joint into view from behind the door.

'Not even if it would mean forgetting you existed,' Sally tried a more pleasant tack, smiling sweetly as she dismissed him.

'See, I don't think any of you –'

'That's enough!' I completely lost my temper, marching to the water's edge, picking up a large, heavy stone and marched back to stand in front of the Capri. 'We've asked you to leave us alone, but now if you don't, I'll put this stone through the bonnet of your car, or through your pig-ugly face.'

'Jesus, Flip, you've gotta learn to relax more, darlin', I was only having some fun.'

'Leave. Now,' Katie said, with fire in her eyes, leaning in to his driver's side window, and Todd, looking from her to me and back again, finally got the message. The tarmac road had recently been resurfaced with a layer of loose chippings, Todd revved his engine and spun his wheels, sending small sharp stones flying in all directions before roaring off up the road, leaving a plume of grey dust in his wake.

Katie walked up to me and put her hand on my shoulder, then gently lifted the stone from my grip. 'It's alright, Flip, he's gone.' She tossed the stone down the banking. It bounced and rolled, gradually slowing down as the mud reached for it, before slipping into the water, sending ripples slowly out across the surface as it disappeared. One small action sending waves out across the whole body of water.

'Why did you bite?'

'I dunno.'

'You never bite.'

'I know, and I don't know. He just pushes my buttons.'

'And not in a good way.'

'Yeuch, fuck me no.' I turned and walked away and tried to ignore the funny looks the others gave me for the rest of that day.

Two days later, Todd Ainsworth was dead.

∞ ∞ ∞

We started fairly early for us that morning, all arriving at Janey's by nine thirty. There'd been rain the previous day when we'd planned to go to the lake, so we were raring to go this morning. Janey wasn't quite ready – nothing new there – and she spent the next fifteen minutes going in and out of her house as she checked whether she'd got spare clothes, something to drink, something to eat and some sun cream. When we finally set off, the day was starting to warm up nicely. At the bottom of Stow Lane, our bikes almost turned left themselves onto Lake Road.

Just out of the village and after the bungalows whose owners mowed their grass verges like their own lawns, we saw a plume of smoke coming from a farm lane further on up the road.

'What the hell is that?' asked Sally, riding on ahead, her bike wobbling along the middle of the road as she accelerated. We moseyed along behind, with little interest in whatever fire some farmer had set the day before. We watched Sally disappear off to the right, presumably down the track, although we weren't yet close enough to see it, so it just looked like she'd disappeared into the hedge. The thin line of smoke rose straight up as we slowly approached, with no sign of Sal returning. Then we heard her scream, a high-pitched scream of pure terror and we moseyed no longer. We could see the turning now as we got close and got there on the double, racing round onto the road, leaning over like we were in the Tour de France peloton. Just up ahead we could easily make out the back of a sky-blue Ford Capri, parked in the middle of the track.

'Oh Jesus, get over here you lot, sharpish!' Sally called back to us, still astride her bike and leaning one hand against the back of the car to steady herself.

Getting closer, the car was less recognisable, with only the rear untouched and the sides looking progressively more charred until we reached the front which was completely black. The frame of the windscreen had buckled and warped, the paint had bubbled and blackened as it boiled during the fire. Sally was off her bike now and walking up to the open driver's window for a better look. She leaned in, then immediately turned away, coughing and retching.

'What is it, Sal? Is someone inside?' I tried to look across, but the acrid smoke and residual heat made my eyes water. I ran around the burnt-out front, aiming for Sal who was puking in the hedgerow.

'Is there someone in there?'

'Oh yeah,' Sally managed between parting with her breakfast in the bushes

'Is he… dead?'

'Oh yeah,' she said, wiping strings of vomit from her face.

Resting my hand on her shoulder I looked across to the car, the smell of burnt plastic and rubber strong in my nostrils. From this side it was very obvious there was a corpse in the driver's seat. Smoke and steam rose from the body and curled and drifted out of the windows. His chest was a charred skeleton, dripping with stuff, and his entire abdomen was missing. Further down, his blackened pelvis sat ghoulishly in the seat amongst the ashes of his thighs. His lower legs, however, were well preserved.

'Is it definitely Todd?' Clara asked, not wanting to even look inside.

'Oh God yeah.' I was staring right at his face, which was now a maniacal caricature of Todd Ainsworth as the heat had made his muscles contract and contort into a hideously twisted grin before melting his eyes to leave empty sockets. The skin was darkened and retracted to expose his teeth, but otherwise intact, and his blackened charcoal tongue lolled from one corner of his mouth.

'Fuck. Off!' exclaimed Clara.

'Oh Jesus, and I threatened him the other day.' A sudden fear gripped me. I'd threatened him with a rock in front of the other girls.

'But you didn't kill him, though, right?' Janey asked, looking at me like Mum would.

'No, of course not.'

'You're sure?'

'I think I would've remembered popping out and killing him, don't you?'

'Right. So what are you worried about?'

'The police. If they know I had a go at him and couldn't stand him…'

'Nobody could stand him – probably not even his Gran – he was a hideous prick and I'm not sorry he's dead. None of us are gonna tell the police you threatened him, are we?' Janey asked, looking around at the others who all nodded their confirmation.

'Thanks guys. Got a bit scared then,' I smiled sheepishly. 'But someone'll have seen the smoke and called them, won't they, so we better make ourselves scarce.'

'That's the second one, though,' said Janey.

'What?'

'The second person burned to death, Clara, in less than two weeks. Old lady Grimshaw, now Todd.'

'The press'll be all over this again.'

'Yeah, that Professor guy'll be back,' Katie added.

'At least he'll be the weirdest guy in the village now.'

'What do you mean?'

'Well, now Todd's dead there's no competition.'

'Sal!'

Chapter 8

— Now —

Janey's Parents

'I was sorry to hear about your mum and dad, Janey,' I said, staring at the dregs of my tea, swirling the sediment around reminded me of the fair when it came to the village and the rides we'd go on – each of us being one of the small particles of tea leaves.

'Yeah, well, it happens. Yours are gone too, right? No biggy.'

'I know but you had to deal with it…'

'By myself? That's nothing new for me, Flip.'

'Can't believe we didn't hear somehow before though. You know – from my parents, Clara's,' Katie added.

'Well, it's a lesson isn't it – staying in touch doesn't just happen by osmosis. We never did and it just fades, doesn't it.'

'What does?' said Sal absently. 'I heard some things years later – do you mind if I ask what happened?' Sal was probing.

'No, it's okay. It's been a long time. Okay, so you remember that they were really heavy smokers?' We all nodded, it was a standing joke that you didn't want a lift in the Pullman-mobile or you'd need a gasmask. Even back then, when it was perfectly reasonable to smoke in a car with your kids, it seemed excessive. 'About five years after you all left for uni, Dad was diagnosed with lung cancer. I don't suppose it was a big surprise, but it still came as a shock, you know. He was still a relatively young, fit man…'

'Sorry, Janes,' I said.

'No it's okay, Flip, really. Anyway, he was going through the treatment side of things and they were quite careful to keep a lot of that away from me. I was away with the fairies at that time, I guess. All treatment for my leg had stopped but the pain was still there and I just bummed around the house – I put on so much weight – got really fat. Anyway, Mam was shouldering all this herself – I knew she was upset at times, but I was never very good at that empathy stuff, and like I say, I wasn't really there.' Janey sat, wincing, as if talking about the pain in her leg was making it hurt now. 'They said it was a result of all the years of smoking and passive smoking because Dad was far worse than Mum for the fags, but I reckon it was the stress and worry that brought it on. She got progressively thinner and more frail after Dad was told he was terminal and she was eventually diagnosed with leukaemia.'

'Oh bloody hell, love.' I put my hand on hers, feeling the whorls and pits of her scarred and twisted skin. For some reason I expected it to be tight and hard, but the skin was soft and warm – just different to mine. Janey pulled her hand away.

'By that time, I'd got myself together a bit more. The internet had started and I was doing some writing. I did some online articles – I guess what would now be called blogging, and I was getting paid a little. So my parents could see that I was getting my life together a bit – I still never went outside, but I guess they could understand that to an extent. So anyway, one night they drove to Willoughby Park, which is somewhere where they used to take me when I was little for walks on my bike and stuff. According to the fire people, it looked like they'd planned to kill themselves by using the exhaust fumes piped into the car with a hose. I guess neither could go on with what was happening to them, and the note they wrote to me said they didn't want me to have a greater burden and be their carer or anything.'

'Oh Janes. Look you don't have to go on – I'm really sorry I brought it up,' Sal looked horrified.

'It's okay, really. It's nice to be able to talk to someone – and I never get the chance to. Not in person, anyway. 'cept the Tesco guy of course. Besides, it has some relevance to now.'

Katie, Sal and I exchanged a look, wondering what that meant exactly. Clara was staring down at her tea, I could see she was tearing up.

'You said the fire brigade found them and it looked like they'd been using a hose…?'

'Yeah, that's right. Dad used the hose from the garden and taped it onto the exhaust pipe of the car, running it in through his slightly open window. But he'd obviously decided that if he was going to die he might as well go out blazing, so he'd lit up and driven there smoking like a chimney – there were loads of fag butts in the ashtray apparently. I guess he'd wanted a last fag as the hose was running and it looks like they both must've been unconscious with it still smouldering.'

'That's carbon monoxide poisoning isn't it?' Katie asked, seemingly unconcerned about the sensitivity of the subject matter. 'Wouldn't that put a cigarette out?'

'Well you'd think so, wouldn't you, but they said as there wasn't an airtight seal around the window – Dad hadn't taped it up –some oxygen would've got in and kept the thing smouldering like an ember, provided that it had fuel. It seems the fuel was Dad's shirt, and then him.'

'Oh my god,' I was feeling pretty numb about this whole thing, and it felt weird just how matter-of-fact Janey was about it. I suppose if you've lived with something every day for twenty-odd years it might get like that, but experiencing it for the first time was very strange. Clara got up and left, closing the bathroom door a few seconds later. Janey looked up and watched her go.

'So the car very gradually caught fire, and they told me it took quite a bit of piecing together what had happened. Like I said before, the funeral was the last time I went out.'

'Janes, I've said it before, but I'm so sorry, lovely. I can't believe how strong you are, you are amazing.' I gave her hand a squeeze again, then let go before she could feel uncomfortable and pull away.

'Janey, you said what happened to your parents has relevance to what's going on now. What do you mean?'

'It's me, it's *us,* K. The Shadow Man got to me, doing all *this,*' she pointed at her leg. 'I'd seen too much, I'd found him out – we all had. But he could never get to you guys – you were scattered across the country, and I guess he wasn't gonna come calling. So he stayed here, tormenting me and everyone else.'

'Hang on, do you think this is our fault for leaving?' asked Katie.

'No, no, God no, I would've left if I could – there's no sense in everyone getting dragged down by this place. By *him*.'

'And do you think the Shadow Man killed your parents?' I asked gently.

'Yes – of course. Terminal illness or not, there's no way Mum and Dad would do that – they'd fight.'

'But what about not being a burden on you?'

'I believe that, but I think they would've set something up – MacMillan nurses or something.' Janey shrugged.

'So they didn't write the note?'

'Yes, Mum did – it was her writing, so unless he can mimic handwriting… But it was him getting inside their heads that did it.'

'He's like the devil.' Clara had returned from the bathroom, her eyes red.

'Yes, yes he is, that's a good shout.'

'Really?' asked Katie. 'As far as that?'

'Why not? He tortured people and killed them in different ways when he was alive. What if, when he's dead, as a spirit or whatever, he's got a lot more freedom to get at people?'

'So is that what he was doing when he burned the village hall down – trying to get to us?' I asked.

'Yes, I think so. Both our mums worked there, didn't they, I think he was trying to get to them to get at us.'

'But why us? Why particularly was he gunning for us?' asked Sal.

'Because we'd seen him, we were standing up to him – challenging him,' Janey said, warming to her subject. 'For two hundred years he's been a cancer in this village, hiding in the shadows with nobody challenging him. But we found him out. We've seen him – he's shown himself to us, and there are no records of that, there are just little snippets and stories from down the years that people round here have attributed to the Shadow Man, as if he's the Bogeyman or something.'

'I still can't remember seeing him or anything like that,' said Sal.

'You will. Give it time, it'll come back.'

'And do you think he escalated from when we started to put two and two together?' I asked.

'Yes, absolutely. I think from the day we saw old lady Grimshaw, and the authorities had all that hocus pocus stuff about spontaneous human combustion.'

'You said there are snippets and stories – how have you got old records about him, Janey, after the village hall went up? What was there left after that?'

'Yeah, wasn't easy. Some of the old historical records from the village were definitely kept in the hall, and some were lost, some not. If it wasn't for the internet, and the main historical records being kept on databases, I wouldn't have had any chance. But, you know, with time on my hands, I could gradually put together a bit of a picture.'

'I read your blog about him before we came,' said Katie.

'Why didn't you mention that before?' I asked. 'Yesterday you said you didn't even remember the Shadow Man.'

'I dunno. I didn't remember. My memory's really been messing with me.'

'That's the point, he does that, that's why we all forgot.'

'And that's what you meant when you said we'd been 'made to forget'?' I said.

'Exactly. That article was from last year – it became a bit like a Masters in the Shadow Man, and I wrote a couple of blogs on how it seemed like his curse, if you like, hung over the place. You've gotta be careful when you write that kind of thing. If you write it too explicitly and people take it at face value then they're gonna think you're a crazy woman. Real life *isn't* a Stephen King novel, right?'

'So why do you think he's back now, after being gone for so long?' I asked.

'Well, first of all 'back' implies that he's been away – I'm not sure he has. I think what we did – finding him out at a time when he was active – let the genie out of the bottle, and that's what's run this place down even more. There used to be more of a community here, but that's all gone and people are just living for convenience. It's like a two-dimensional village in a movie that gets dismantled when filming stops. And I think the Shadow Man feeds off it. A solid community could resist something creeping in and getting into people's heads, but not here.'

'And now he's got a taste for it?' Katie asked.

'I think so, the death and destruction. He's out there and he's watching. I feel like he's growing, taking over, feeding off people.'

'How?'

'I dunno, it's just the feeling I get. And then there's us. I think he's toying with us. Like I said, we're the first people who ever challenged him, so he's relishing it – it's like a game.'

'There's a lot of stuff in there Janes. A lot of ideas, and –'

'Yeah, we can't corroborate any of it, it's all ideas, and that's why you've gotta be careful who you tell them to otherwise you're a nutcase. But we've all seen him, and so you are all my fellow nutcases.'

'Okay so, assuming that all of that is the case,' said Katie, 'How do we stop him?'

'Well, unsurprisingly, I've given this more thought than anything else. I think we need to give him what he wants.'

'Which is?'

'Us.'

Chapter 9

— Then —

Incoming

Did we get 'in bother' that summer as my mum used to say?

In a word, yes.

Not like kids do these days, of course, and nothing bad. I remember going up to see Kelly Bridgewater one day. She lived up on the hill, in one of the big new houses with views out over the Vale. She wasn't part of our little gang, so we didn't often visit her. We played tennis in her cul-de-sac and I smashed a ball over a fence, into the garden of the house opposite. The stomach-sinking sound of breaking glass soon followed, and we legged it pronto. For weeks I was convinced the old guy who lived there would find out who the vandal was and turn up at my house. That's about the level of the trouble we got into.

We rode down the hill like our lives depended on it, almost expecting to hear a cacophony of sirens approaching, overtaking us and cordoning off the road for our Butch and Sundance moment. The wind was in our hair, and we squinted against the force of the air against our eyes, but still they watered, so we cried and laughed at the same time, at breakneck speed down the hill.

$$\infty \quad \infty \quad \infty$$

That day wasn't unlike this. We'd been up the hill again, but this time to see our friend Leigh Roach. Fish wasn't allowed to go to the lake, so we often used to go up to hers instead, and today her mum had put out a paddling pool, the hosepipe and water pistols for us to mess around with. We'd spent the day lazing around punctuated by demented water fights and now we were racing down the hill again. From out of nowhere we had bogeys at three and nine o'clock. Lee Jenkins and Mark Drudge had sped up behind us on their bigger Grifters, outflanking us as we pelted down the narrow lane. They were penning us in like herding sheep, and I looked behind to see Luke Michael Lewis cruising up from behind, almost nudging his way through the others to inch up alongside me at the front, like using wide shoulders to wade through a queue.

'Well Flip, when are you going to give me that blow job I've been asking for?' he leered, his face just inches from mine – the bike helmet not invented back then.

'I'd rather do your granddad, Luke Lewis. But then, who the hell calls their kid Luke Lewis?' I swerved away to avoid a manhole cover, my front wheel wobbling alarmingly as it hit the patched tarmac around it, before I swerved back in line with my tormentor. 'It's as bad as William Williams. You're a reduplicant.'

'He's always struck me as one, Flip,' shouted Katie.

'Fuck you. What are you calling me?'

'Doesn't matter, you wouldn't understand.'

'It's Luke Michael Lewis you bitch, and you know it,' he said through gritted teeth, it was always really easy to wind him up. 'Perhaps I should drag you off down to the lake right now – just the two of us. Let's see how clever you are then.'

'Always cleverer than you, Dumbo, always cleverer.'

'Oh you little cow –' he reached across to grab my shoulder, but I weaved away again, ducking at the last moment, causing him to overstretch, with the inevitable loss of balance. I'd leaned my bike over too much and was heading straight for the almost vertical grassy bank at terminal velocity, my tyres biting hard and complaining. I threw myself over in the opposite direction, leaning downhill, trying to take the bike round before it hit the bank, but there was no way of stopping it. My front wheel hit the steep compacted soil, for a second catching in the earth, threatening to flip the bike up into the air, but then digging in and shredding soil and stones from the unstable slope beneath the tufts of grass as the tyre climbed up, plumes of dust spewing out from behind me like smoke. By the time my back wheel joined it I was horizontal, riding along the bank like I was in a 'wall of death' act in the circus. I turned to look over my shoulder and saw the result of Lewis' over-stretching. He and the bike were starting to move in opposite directions, the bike dropping away from him, halfway down before those behind realised what was happening and took evasive action. Lewis was falling to the side, but the handlebars were twisting the front wheel under him, and suddenly the wheel locked, flipping the bike. He was catapulted violently into the air, summersaulting over like a rag doll before managing to break his fall onto the road with his face. My pace had slowed and I rode down off the bank and onto the tarmac of the lane once more, continuing to look over my shoulder. My enduring memory of that day is of seeing him recede into the distance, propped up on one hand with blood pouring from his chin, a huge flap of skin underneath opening out like a second mouth. He was like a gore-drenched two-mouthed monster from a sci-fi film, screaming. 'You're fucking dead, you bitch! You hear me? I'm gonna fucking kill you!'

We lay low for a few days – speaking on the phone or visiting each other's houses by bike, but never riding round as a group. I heard that Lewis had to go to hospital to have stitches in his chin.

These memories were returning to me in sudden bursts. Things I hadn't thought about in decades, about home and friends and school. The cliques and groups the social pecking order, the stuff I was always telling my own kids they should ignore and not get involved with. No wonder they never talked to me about this stuff. I'd forgotten what it was like, how it felt, the way you could get your head kicked in for what, as an adult, looked like nothing.

I don't really remember how we fell foul of his stupid little gang. He'd become used to people being deferent around him, getting out of his way and paying him 'due' respect. He'd been a dickhead at junior school, but had just thrown his weight around, bumping into people, and shoving them out of his way. Lewis had obviously met some other like-minded folks when we went to comp in Dayden, lads he could influence and rule over like a gang leader, like Mark Drudge and Lee Jenkins. He also grew a harem of females that would worship at his feet – or anywhere else he told them to, presumably – and we weren't like that. We tended to ignore him and people like him, like they didn't matter, like they had no relevance to us and didn't exist. I guess that's what was infuriating to someone like him – someone who wanted to exert control and create fear in others.

Or something.

He'd become a bully, lording it at school with his mates, threatening little kids – not stealing dinner money or anything like that, just being a presence and deciding to pick on someone for the sake of it. He and his gang would often wander across the playground, right across a game of football or keepy-uppy, bringing the game to a standstill. They'd strut around in front of the younger children in their Mod jackets, maybe shoving a couple of them, sometimes terrifying one by grabbing them and using their favourite phrase, 'I want you, don't I?' as if their protection racket had the child on a bullying hit-list. After they'd suitably ruined the game, they'd wander off to bother the next group. Sometimes they'd encounter one of the other small groups of bullies who did the same, and a fight would inevitably ensue, which were always entertaining. Maybe once a week someone would lash out at someone else and the call of 'Fight! Fight! Fight! Fight!' would go up. If you were 'lucky', it would happen in front of you and the ring of kids would form with you in the front row seats. More usually, it would happen somewhere else and we'd just watch from a distance as a small stadium of children formed, with those at the back jumping up to get onto the backs of those in front to see the action. 'The action' was usually pretty poor – all handbags and holding each other – like watching two has-been heavyweight fighters come out of retirement for one last payday. The spectacle would also quickly bring some teachers to break it up, before the protagonists were led away for a talking-to from the Head.

The real disagreements were settled elsewhere, without the crowds and the hype. We were walking down a corridor near the gym one day after lunch, just hanging around with nothing to do. Around the corner in front of us came two boys running at speed. The one behind grabbed the other one, pulling him to a halt and swinging three or four vicious punches at his face, while the other could only raise his hands in self-defence. Just like that it was over, and the victor quickly walked off to re-join his friends who had just arrived on the scene, presumably after being part of the ambush for this particular prey. Nose pouring blood onto his shirt, the beaten boy got to his feet, angrily pushing us out of the way before storming off, etiquette demanding that we not make eye contact to avoid a 'What are you looking at?' moment.

Now, during the summer holidays, there was no reason why we should bump into him, the village was big enough for us to be able to keep our distance, but I knew he'd be out there looking for us. For me. Wanting his revenge. He was crazy, and he was a bully, so how badly would he want to mess me up?

Chapter 10

— Then —

Royal Game Soup

What a ridiculous name I'm saddled with. Eveline and Ronald Dover aren't too bad, really. There are worse surnames to have, they just needed to take a little care with the Christian names they gave their kids. Except they didn't. But Philippa Dover? Oh, what fun the kids in school had with that. Flip' Dover was a stalwart along with a dozen more besides. And my brother Raymond… it might've needed more work but they usually just called him Ben.

Ray was off to university in Manchester that autumn. Beforehand, he and his friends had decided to go camping, choosing the Yorkshire Dales as a picturesque and relatively close destination should anything go awry. Mum and Dad had bought him a tent for his birthday and he'd been working through the summer holidays so he could buy the rest of the gear he'd need. I remember when he packed it all up into his blue Mark II Escort one sunny Saturday morning, and drove off for a planned week of heavy drinking, leching at local girls and poor personal hygiene.

By lunchtime on Monday he was back.

∞ ∞ ∞

Regardless of the outside temperature, a hearty soup was not unusual for the summer lunch menu chez Dover, despite all the windows and doors being thrown open due to the heat. We obviously couldn't sit down to anything like a salad because, to mum, a salad entailed nothing but slices of tomato and cucumber. That didn't constitute a meal. So lunch was either soup or sandwiches as far as she was concerned, and we'd 'enjoyed' tinned salmon sandwiches the Friday before.

We sat down to eat in the dining room, the silence only broken by the sound of spoons scraping bowls and Dad and I trying not to look at each other when we were slurping our soup.

'There's some rum stuff going on that's for sure,' Dad said into his bowl, as if he was talking to himself.

'Oh?' I wasn't sure what he might be getting at but hoped it wasn't anything we'd done.

'Two people burning to death within half a mile of each other doesn't strike you as odd, Flip?'

'I spose it does, when you say it like that.'

'And that professor fella on the telly saying it's spontaneous combustion. To me, that's just a load o' rubbish.'

'What do you think's going on?'

'Well I don't know. But this sort of thing just can't be a coincidence, can it? You just be careful when you're out and about with your little gang.'

'Is this where you tell me not to talk to strangers, Dad?'

'Aye it is, and there's nowt wrong with that. Good advice that. You stick together you girls. You'll be safe then.' Dad returned to his soup in a 'here endeth the lesson' moment.

We all heard the sound of a car screeching to a halt on the driveway, the engine revving one last time before it was cut off. Then the door slammed. Ray stormed into the dining room.

'Did you have a nice time, Ray, love? You're back sooner than I thought. How was the weather? Did you manage to keep warm? How was the tent?' Mum always fired questions at you so you felt like someone being machine-gunned in a war film.

'Fucking pissed it down the whole fucking time!' Ray angrily ran up the stairs to his bedroom. I was glad I hadn't sat opposite Dad, because he would've pebble-dashed my white 'Relax' t-shirt with Baxter's Royal Game Soup after Ray's outburst. It was the first and last time I heard Ray swear in front of Dad, and I instantly worried for him when my father slowly and calmly rose from his chair to leave the table, fury in his eyes. I didn't hear all the ensuing argument, but I did hear raised voices and Dad using terms never to be repeated.

Ray repeated his earlier weather report to me after lunch and explained that it had rained so hard that water had poured into the tent, soaking him and his friends to the skin. All their gear had been soaked-through too, their sleeping bags and spare clothes, and whilst they'd tried to tough it out, a night shivering in a sopping-wet sleeping bag was the last straw. Hence their return and Ray's foul mood. As if to reinforce this, he smelled like a wet dog that had been marinating in pond water for a couple of days.

Ray and Dad pitched the tent in the garage to let it dry out, and hung all the other gear on strip-lights, stepladders, and pieces of wood that Dad always kept in there for some imaginary job that he would never do. I didn't even ask if I could take the new camping stove down to the lake – Ray was never going to use it again, and I was sure he didn't have an inventory for half of this stuff. So equipment disappeared, a bit at a time; torches, tent pegs to stop our stuff getting blown around on the banking, dry bags that we used to store our non-perishable gear in the trees behind the lake to save carrying back and forth. You couldn't say we weren't resourceful, when it came to 'stealing' stuff.

Chapter 11

— Then —

Trespassers

We often brought alcohol with us to the lake. A helpful brother might buy us some beer from the shop, or Janey might 'borrow' some vodka from her mum. Today we'd passed the bottle around, sipping it in the heat on an empty stomach and soon feeling tipsy. Then Janey fired up the cooking stove.

'Tea everyone,' Janey called after a few minutes as the water began to boil. I'd been lounging in the sun while the others had been splashing around in the lagoon. Janey was usually in charge of tea or coffee. We sat around her in a circle and watched as she arranged some plastic cups that I'd also liberated from Ray's belongings, and half-filled each with the steaming water from the pan.

'What's this?' Katie asked.

'Mushroom tea,' Janey replied.

'Oh fuck off, I hate mushrooms,' exclaimed Clara, about to pour the brew away.

'You'll like these. They're magic mushrooms.'

'What?'

'You know, magic mushrooms – gets you off your face.'

'Fucking hell. How do you know about this stuff?'

'They have this thing now called reading, in the library, you know?'

'Is it safe?' I asked, warily sniffing the musty smelling drink.

'Yes definitely – picked some last time and tried them in tea at home – it's very weird, but amazing. Like being drunk without the need to piss all the time.'

'Where the hell did you find them?' Clara was not going to be convinced anytime soon.

'Over there,' she pointed in the direction of the nettle patch and the barn skeleton. 'On the grassy bank as it slopes away – it's muddy and shaded by the trees. There were loads.'

'Okay-y,' Katie said then immediately took a sip. 'Fuck,' she spat, 'What is this, it's like dog shit tea?'

'It's not the nicest, I'll give you that.'

'Bottoms up,' I raised my cup in a mock toast, took a sip of the earthy-tasting water then drained the rest, including some of the residue in the bottom. 'Are you s'posed to eat the mushrooms in the bottom?' I asked Janey, but she shrugged and continued to sip her drink.

It took a while for everyone to empty their cups and flop back on the grass to stare at the sky. I studied the vapour trails left behind by aircraft flying who-knew-where. The warmth of the sun melted my naked body.

The tension, the hassle, the everyday annoyances were massaged away by the heat washing over me from the caress of the wind. I gave myself up to it and became part of the yellow glow all around me. I felt like a speck of dust, blowing around a vast desert, so inconsequential was I in the universal scheme of things. I had the same feelings when laying on my back on the lawn staring up at the stars in the dead of night – a time when you can really see the universe laid out in front of you – all that was stopping you going exploring was mankind's physical limitations. One day someone will be laying down on her lawn looking up at the stars, then she'll jump into a ship and fly right up there amongst them.

One day.

I dozed dreamily, barely aware of the others around me, the sound of wildfowl quietly going about their business with the odd flapping of wings or a call to a fellow lake dweller. The wind itself was a friend, touching my hair, stroking over me, always checking I was okay and keeping the temperature just right. My metaphysical oneness with both the breeze and the cosmos relaxed me as much as I could ever remember. Time stood still and the world around us drifted away. *I* drifted away, falling backwards through the bank, through the lake and the earth, spiralling down and away into the void, my awareness fading in and out for a while, almost breaking the surface before dropping away again.

I'm not sure how long I slept.

My consciousness returned. The warmth remained on my skin, and I was so hot that I thought I should maybe take a dip to cool off. But that wasn't why I'd awakened. There was bird movement on the lake – the busy sounds of landing and taking off – like an avian Heathrow airport. But that wouldn't have disturbed me either.

Then I recognised the sound in the background.

Voices.

Boys talking loudly – not yet so close that I could understand what they were saying, but definitely getting closer. I sat bolt upright and looked around at my friends, realising our vulnerability and more importantly, the likelihood of embarrassment.

'Girls,' I said in a stage whisper, but received no response. 'Hey, you lot!' I hissed with increased volume and urgency. 'Someone's coming.'

'Not anywhere near me, he isn't,' said Katie sitting upright, not attempting to hide her nakedness. 'Who?'

'Dunno. Boys, though.'

'Shit, we better get dressed – get the others up.'

We quickly roused the other three and pulled on our clothes, all the while listening to what sounded like three or four voices getting ever closer. We ran to retrieve our bikes, peering round the corner of the barn skeleton to see if we could see anyone. Just beyond the barn and a big oak, I could see the approaching figures shimmering through the heat haze, turning animatedly to talk to one other, shoving each other and picking up handfuls of grass to push down each other's shirts. They were walking along the path having presumably left their bikes at the start of the track, and were so pre-occupied they didn't see me.

'Quick, they're nearly here – let's get going,' I whispered. We grabbed our bikes and ran back with them to our camp, picking up bags, towels and water bottles before disappearing into the brush. 'Shit,' I said, realising that we'd flattened the grass on the bank. It might've given away that someone had been there. I burst back out from our cover position.

'Flip, what the fuck are you doing, come back,' Katie hissed.

I did the lake equivalent of plumping the cushions up at the end of a party to tell everyone to go home. I bent and roughed the grass up, disguising that we'd been there. I started at the far end and slowly walked backwards, ending at the treeline and looking at my work before disappearing again. The grass looked terrible but it might fool those idiots.

The others had gone on ahead, pushing their bikes down into a dip which was a soak-away from the lake above, the slope lined by fallen tree trunks rotting away, covered in lichens and algae. I collected my bike, which I'd thrown to one side before running back to pimp the grass, and slowly started pushing it along. With every revolution of the back wheel, the hub clicked and ticked, making what must've been the loudest noises known to man. It seemed like the unnatural metallic sounds echoed around the trees and were surely being broadcast out to the approaching boys, giving us away. I lifted the bike by the seat, raising the rear wheel from the ground and ran as quietly as I could down the slope, the handlebars steering precariously until the front wheel caught in a tree root and the bike flipped us both to the ground. The others looked back at me with alarm as we heard the voices of the boys, close now, on the other side of the leafy screen. Holding my finger to my lips was the most stupidly obvious thing to do, but it made us all stare at each other and we silently squatted down as one to make us less visible should they burst through the trees. My plumping of the grass must've worked because they didn't take any notice of where we'd camped. A couple of them paddled in the shallow water, stepping around reed beds and clumps of bulrushes. One of them did this without realising the water suddenly got deep at the start of the lagoon and went in up to his waist.

'Fuck! Fuck this place. Fuck! Get me out of here, will you?' His friends hauled him out of the water, laughing hard at his misfortune, and he continued to use the f-word more liberally than Clara and Katie put together.

'Simone said that those girls come out here,' said one.

'Who?'

'You know, Katie Edwards and her stupid mates. The ones that fucked you up, Luke.'

'I know that, obviously, that's why we're here, you knob. Who the fuck is Simone?'

'Jenk's sister. She talks to 'em. She knows that Philippa.'

'I'd fuck her up if she was here. She ain't doing that to me, the bitch. I'd show her. That'd show her.' He turned to his friends and I could see through a gap in the leaves that he was grabbing his crotch and thrusting it at them. 'Oh yeah, I'd teach her something.'

'This place is a dump, though. All this mud and weed and fucking birds.' I couldn't see who'd said it and didn't know the gang well enough to recognise their voices. 'Glad you've got a pool, Luke.'

'Fucking right, much rather be at mine having a swim than here.' Luke's parents had money, and were the first people in the village to build their own swimming pool.

The boys walked past the bank where we were hiding and out of sight – they must've been walking across the short spur of land that ended in the tree with the rope swing. I moved across the dip, staying in a crouch and saw them again through the bushes at the beach on the far side. We never went to the far beach because it was always noisy with birds and at over halfway round the lake you were almost in sight of the farmhouse, and you certainly were if the farmer was in any of his outbuildings. Without looking back, I raised my hand so the others would know to stay as they were. The boys must've decided to camp there and have a swim, because they all started to strip off, and I got my first glimpse of adolescent manhood. I slowly backed away as they shouted and screamed at the cool water when they went in, picking up my bike, knowing that we could escape under the cover of the racket they were making.

'Go, go,' I said in another loud-as-I-dare whisper, following the others as they clambered up the steep bank on the far side of the copse, up and out onto a narrow path bisecting the hill – probably an animal trail – where the others waited for me.

'Close run thing?'

'Not really, Janes, once they started posing with their dicks out it was easy to get away.'

'Ooh, let's see,' said Katie.

'Haven't you seen them all already?'

'Nice.'

'Let's get out of here,' I said. 'There's only so long idiots like that are gonna spend down here before getting bored.' Forced to move in single file, we pushed our bikes along the trail, occasionally having to negotiate brambles or large patches of nettles. The trail continued to rise and we could see the steep bank to our left was fenced off above us.

'Must be the top lake,' said Janey looking up at the chain link.

'It's funny how we've never come up here,' Katie added.

After a further hundred yards or so the trail reached the top of the bank and became a wider path, revealing a small lake on the other side of the fence, almost completely hidden by undergrowth. One of the fence panels had partly fallen and the chains had ripped, leaving a gap big enough for us to go through. So we all did.

'Hold the frigging wire back a bit more would you, Flip? I can't squeeze through.' Katie just managed to fit through the gap as I pulled the chain-link fence back on itself, the cold rusted metal digging into my fingers. We pushed through the wall of brambles and nettles and there in front of us was the top lake. The third of the three lakes made by the quarrying company in the seventies it was small and shallow, not much bigger than a pond, with wide muddy banks and squadrons of mosquitos buzzing around.

'What's that smell, it's like something's died in there?' Katie asked.

'Don't think it's that, I think the water's just stagnant. Look at all the mozzies flying around,' Janey pointed to the clouds of flies over the water.

We walked around the periphery, arms waving wildly to keep the insects away. Above the far bank, a flattened plateau of compacted gravel and dust opened out, at the back of which was a squat zinc shed like a double garage. The zinc sheets were rusted and some had fallen away, and the roller shutter doors were half open. We ducked underneath and went inside. The dusty workshop smelled of oil and fuel. Workbenches were cluttered with piles of boxes containing machine parts, shelves were overloaded and buckled under the weight of their contents. There was stuff everywhere.

'What was this place?' Katie wondered aloud as she stepped over a collapsed shelving unit.

'Must be the garage they used when they were quarrying,' I replied.

'Garage?' Sal was looking up through gaps in the zinc wall at a large rusted tank outside.

'For their machines – diggers and stuff. They can't just take one of them to Jenkins' garage in the village can they?' said Janey.

'They've just piled all this stuff up then left. That's odd,' I said, poking around in boxes.

'I guess if they shut down pretty quickly they would leave stuff.'

Clara stepped outside, her shoes crunching on the hard-core. 'Come and look at this, you lot,' she called. Taking care where we stepped we emerged into the sunshine and looked across at Clara, who was standing halfway between the workshop and the lake. The gravel surface here was more uneven and rocky, with several large boulders breaking through the hard-core. Between these stones the ground disappeared into a large hole.

'What the hell is that?' Katie asked.

'A sink hole, maybe' replied Janey. 'It's where the ground just opens up and swallows whatever was above. You get it in limestone, sometimes, because it dissolves quite easily.'

'How the hell do you know this stuff, nerd-girl?' Katie playfully punched her on the shoulder and Janey looked uncomfortable to be the centre of attention.

'Actually it's not,' said Janey, contradicting herself, walking in front of Clara, approaching the hole.

'Janey,' I called after her, worried the ground might not be stable.

'It's a cave.' Janey stood with her toes hanging over the edge of the hole, peering down into the darkness. We joined her and sure enough could see that after a drop of about five feet, there was a definite floor that sloped downwards to disappear under the ground. Janey pulled a torch from her backpack – there was little she didn't carry with her on days at the lake – and took a step out over the edge.

'Janey, no!' I cried, but it was no use, Janey stepped off and landed with a thud on the dusty floor below – the top of her head protruding above ground. With a click her torch came on, illuminating a narrow circle in front of her.

'It's okay – *I'm* okay!' she smiled. 'There's definitely a bigger cavern down here, this is like an entrance hall.' She walked forwards, following the torch beam.

'Yeah but don't go –' The torch light disappeared as Janey ventured underground. '– any further. Talk to your bloody self, Flip,' I said, exasperated.

'Come on then, sisters together,' said Katie, lowering herself in a more ankle friendly fashion over the side of the hole. Soon we were all peering through the darkness and the dust into the gloom of the big cavern.

'Through here,' Janey said as she set the torch on the floor, standing it on end and pulling the middle up to turn it into a lantern. The room was bathed in a harsh blue-white light. The cave was the size of a large living room, with a domed roof and curved walls reaching down to the floor. In the far corner, there was another hole, going deeper underground.

'What the hell?' Sally was looking at the walls, where there were etchings and rough drawings. Drawings of monsters and flames, of people next to fires or standing over them. Towards the middle of the room, slightly nearer the mouth of the cave, was a pile of ash, and the earth around it was blackened. Next to it was a pile of bones.

'It's the Shadow Man,' said Janey, matter-of-factly.

'The what?' replied Katie.

'I've been reading about Lincolnshire legends, and there's one from here.' Janey seemed a little far away, as if in a trance, her voice sounding different somehow. Maybe she was concentrating to remember what she'd read. 'It's about Laurendon. When it was just farming folk living on the hill, working on the local landowners' estates.'

'When are we talking, Janes?' I asked as she squatted down by the lantern.

'The village has been around for a really long time but this story goes back to the late seventeen hundreds, Flip. I don't know how many houses there were back then but I'm guessing it was dozens, maybe a few hundred, but not thousands. There was a pond, though.'

'So what happened?' I asked, trying to keep Janey focused as she looked around. *What the hell was wrong with her?*

'Kids started to go missing. Taken from their homes and never seen again. And apparently there were some cases where people got burned. Mysteriously. Just like now. There was this guy, William Tullock. He was a bit of an oddball. There wasn't a police force or anything but the local magistrate led a group of people – vigilantes I s'pose – who searched everyone's houses. At Tullock's place they found things belonging to the missing kids.'

'You read all this?' asked Katie.

'So it was him?' I asked.

'The magistrates found him guilty and burned him at the stake.'

'Jesus,' said Sal.

'Did bad things stop happening?'

'Yep, it seems like they got him.'

'You said it was the Shadow Man?' asked Katie.

'It's what they called him – the village children. They said that the Shadow Man would come to get you, to take you away and burn you to ash. They even came up with a rhyme to protect themselves. They reckoned that singing it would protect them from him.'

'Wonder how it went?' said Sally as she looked around.

'I can remember it if you want to hear?' Janey seemed a lot less dreamy now.

'Go on then.'

The Shadow Man comes out at night
The Shadow Man in plain sight
The Shadow Man is gone by dawn
Taking souls for us to mourn

The Shadow Man prowls around
Without noise, without a sound
And if he should catch your eye
Then you know you're going to die

The Shadow Man haunts our home
You're safe until the sun goes down
The Shadow Man will wait his turn
To hold you close and make you burn.'

'Shit, that's as scary as Ring-a-ring-a-roses,' Katie was looking at the hole in the far corner of the cave. 'Let's have a look down here.'

'Okay, can I have the torch?' I picked up the chunky light, pushing down on the top to turn it back from a lantern to a torch, the beam dancing wildly around the walls as our shadows were thrown around. I bent forward and shone it into the hole – it looked like a drop of about three feet before the cavern opened up further down. I sat on the edge and slid forward and down to the ledge below, taking the torch with me. 'Sorry guys, it's gonna go dark.'

'Yeah, thanks a lot.' Katie mimicked a *Scooby Doo* evil laugh.

'That isn't even remotely funny,' said Clara.

'Who said that?'

'Still not fucking funny.'

The cavern opened out and looked more like a proper cave than a weird living room. The array of stalactites just above my head dropped mineral filtered water onto the floor below, creating corresponding stalagmites. It was the same height as the cave above but about three times as long, with the wet floor sloping down towards the far end, the humidity making it hard to breathe. The smell down here was worse – it smelled like something had died, the stench of decay and rotting flesh catching at the back of my throat, almost making me gag.

'How is it down there, Flip?'

'It stinks, smells like something rotten.'

I walked down the slope toward the far end of the cave to where I could see a dark shadow, concentrating hard to keep my footing on the wet stone, my fake-Converse threatened to slip at any moment. As I approached, the torch showed it was a round hole about ten feet across, with water in the bottom about ten feet below.

'There's a stagnant pool at the bottom here,' I called back, my voice echoing. 'Really stinks. But there's also some light.' The murky water below was illuminated to a degree, as if someone had put a pond light on the bottom.

'Could it be coming in from the lake outside – is there a tunnel between them?' Janey's voice echoed down.

'Dunno and I'm not jumping in to find out. Okay, this is officially the weirdest thing I've ever done and I'm coming back now.'

'Good, hurry up with the bloody torch.'

'You're all self, Clara.' I'd reached the step and clambered up, swearing as I hit my head on the overhang, forgetting how little space I had. I handed the torch to someone and took the other proffered hands to help me scramble back out.

'Look over here.' Janey had gone into the opposite corner to the hole in the first cave and was squatting down. 'See these?' She was pointing at something on the floor. 'There are brackets bolted into the floor. They're rusty and look old, really old.'

'What do you think they are?' I bent down to join her.

'Not wanting to jump to conclusions, they could be anything. But why would you bolt some metal brackets into the floor of a cave? Unless you were hiding here. Look at the fire and the rabbit bones or whatever they are – somebody was laying low in here.'

'They can't date back that far anyone could've come in here and left them.'

'Maybe. And did the cave paintings while they were down here as well, perhaps?'

'Point taken. The quarry and the lakes are recent – so what was here before?'

'I'm guessing it must've been a cave at the top of this rise. There was plenty of rolling farmland here, maybe it was just too stony to farm this bit and they ignored whatever cave was here. The history book said they couldn't find Tullock when they raided his place. I can't remember, but I don't think it said how long it took to find him, but it implied it was a while – maybe a few weeks I'm guessing.'

'And he was holed-up here?' I said, nodding.

'Well, let's not get ahead of ourselves – all of a sudden this day out is turning into some kind of Hardy Boys and Nancy Drew mystery,' Katie wasn't convinced. 'Doesn't this all seem a bit convenient – we discover a cave, and all of a sudden there's a local legend that nobody's heard of and the two are linked and I don't fucking know but it just seems –'

'I'm not making this shit up – I'll show you the fucking book, K, I *have* looked into this. Just because people are ignorant of their own local history doesn't mean that bad shit couldn't have happened.'

'Yes, Janey, I know, and I wasn't saying that I thought your story was wrong or anything. Quite frankly I dunno what I was saying. Sorry if I put my fucking foot in it. I dunno, it's all a bit weird.'

'It's okay. It's definitely weird.'

'Do you think this Tullock guy really was the Shadow Man?' Katie asked to make the peace. 'Or did they fit him up?'

'There can't have been a lot of people round here who, down the years, are going to do cave paintings of people being burned alive, can there?'

'And those bolts? I know you've got an idea – can see it in your face.'

'What if he brought the children here – to kill them? What if he chained them up there and did whatever the fuck he did?' We all looked from the bolts and brackets to the fireplace and the small pile of bones. They'd looked like rabbit bones at first glance. But what if they were something else?

'So that was two hundred-odd years ago. What do you think is happening now?' said Katie.

'What do you mean?' Janey's eyes met with ours.

'Well, they found Tullock guilty. He's obviously dead. But now there're people being burned in the village. Is somebody copying him or something?'

'Either there's some kind of copycat setting people on fire, or somehow the Shadow Man is still here. Tullock never went away.'

'They burnt him at the stake and he'd be, like, two hundred and fifty fucking years old,' said Katie, our common-sense barometer.

'I don't mean him, knobhead, I mean his spirit, his essence, his –'

'You're going to say evil aren't you?' said Sally, in an accusing tone.

'Yes, why the hell not?'

'Because it's not fucking possible, that's why. The spirit of a long dead kiddy-fiddler doesn't just come back. This isn't a horror novel. How would it – a ghost maybe – are we believing in ghosts now?'

'I do,' Janey said.

'You fucking would.'

'Hey, calm down guys, let's not get our hair-off. What do you really mean, Janey?' Once again I found myself the peacemaker.

'Plenty of people believe in the soul, right? The essence that is you, that turns this,' she pulled on the skin of her cheek, 'into *us*. You go to church don't you, Clara?'

'Yeah, but I don't choose to.'

'So you don't believe in God?'

'Well, yeah I do. I suppose. I've never really thought about it like that.'

'So you believe in the soul then – going up to heaven when you die and all that?'

'Yeah. Think so,' Clara blushed. She'd never really discussed her faith with us before. Now was the weirdest time to be doing it.

'So let's just say there is a soul, then. What if there was a soul so bad, so evil, if you wanna use that, that it stays around, long after the body is dead. What if it didn't go anywhere – Tullock's soul. What if it's just *here?*'

'So you're saying Laurendon is *evil?*' asked Katie, sounding a little less confident and acerbic than she had before.

'I dunno, and you could say that sounds like a load of bollocks. But if it isn't that. Just what the hell is going on?'

Chapter 12

— Now —

Something's Out There

'Somethings out there,' said Janey.

'What?' asked Katie.

'I dunno, I've just got a feeling.'

'Sure it's not the menopause?' Clara asked.

'Fuck off, Clara. Don't you ever have that feeling, though, that someone is watching you and maybe transmitting your every move back to a higher power? Everyone's had that feeling of being watched – surely...' Janey looked at us for some encouragement.

'That's just paranoia though,' said Sal. Janey gave an exasperated sigh.

'Or maybe it's because we were kids— young and stupid and knowing nothing of the world and some stuff happened to us and our memories of it have just got fucked up over time,' Katie offered another explanation.

'Except our memories have only just returned – we didn't remember anything until a week or two back and now all of a sudden we do, so it can't be that our memories have got twisted over time,' Janey reasoned.

'By 'something' I take it you mean the Shadow Man?' I joined the debate.

'None other.'

'So why are we here? What was the point of us coming back here?'

'Thanks very much.'

'You know I don't mean that Janey Janes, it's been brilliant to see you, all of you, it's been so good to catch up – I wish we'd stayed in touch. But, apart from to support you, why have we come back here, now – to what end?' I asked.

'To find out what really went on back then. To work out what we did, to organise our memories into some kind of order and put together a story that explains what, right now, is a bit of a mystery,' Janey summarised.

'Oh my fucking God, you've grown up into Velma from *Scooby Doo*,' said Clara.

'And I can't see anything without my glasses.'

'Okay, I've just gotta ask one thing though. You know. For the record,' said Sal, her most serious face on.

'Here we go,' said Katie.

'You didn't really kill him, did you, Flip?'

'Who?'

'Todd.'

'No! Of course I didn't. What the fuck?'

'Okay, I know, I know. Just checking.'

'Bloody hell, Sal, you haven't changed, you still say the stupidest stuff.'

'I bet I'm not the only one who just wanted to check,' replied Sal, slightly offended.

'Okay, so what next?' Katie quickly changed the subject.

'We go to the lake,' I said.

'Why?'

'Because you said it yourself. We could've all got together on Skype or Facetime, but we didn't. We're here in person. And the difference about being here in person is that we can go and see things. The lake dominates our memories, it's where so much happened that we can remember and probably more that we can't. Let's go out there.'

'But why? It was thirty years ago,' Katie held her arms out wide and shrugged.

'Do you want to carry on living with these dreams and memories– half a story of something that might have happened? Going there might jog our memories some more, it might make us remember even more stuff, trigger some things – I don't know – but it's gotta be worth a go.'

'And if it does nothing?'

'Then we can start to think that maybe it's not related to the lake, maybe we've developed some subconscious fixation and it's really got nothing to do with it.'

'That's settled then, tomorrow we go to the lake.'

'You coming Janey?' Clara asked.

'No, sorry, I can't. There's only one way I'll ever leave this house again.'

'What? How? I don't under–,' Sal looked confused and then reality dawned. 'Oh, right, duh. I get it. There's nothing like being morbid, is there.'

'We'll come straight back here afterwards and let you know everything we find,' I promised.

'I expect you to be my eyes and ears.'

∞ ∞ ∞

'Right. No messing about, we're having takeaway tonight!' I said, raising a small cheer from the others. All apart from Janey.

'I was gonna make a chilli – I've got some mince to defrost. I don't feel like I've looked after you very much since you've come home.' She did look a little hurt.

'You've been manning HQ, Janes.' I said, supportively, 'Besides, you've stuffed us full of tea, cake, biscuits, I don't see what else you could've done.'

'Should we really be saying 'manning' nearly two decades into the twenty-first century?' asked Katie, her eyebrows raised.

'Stick your HR up your arse, love.' I turned back to Janey. 'Anyway, this way, there's no tidying up and no pans to wash.'

'True.' Janey nodded in agreement.

'Right. Me and Sal can go. Chen – shift your arse.' I grabbed my keys from the worktop.

'Who died and left you in charge?' she said, smiling.

'Talk to HR over there later.' Sal and I left the dilapidated bungalow and climbed into my car.

'So I take it your folks don't run the restaurant any more,' I said as we pulled away from the kerb, 'Or otherwise you'd be staying with them.'

'Oh, God, no. No, Dad sold up about ten years ago. They moved out to Milton Keynes. He died three years ago and mum the following year. They got it right, they had a good life and a good retirement in the end.'

'What on earth made them open a restaurant here anyway, I've always wondered.'

'That was Grandad's idea. He lived in Sheffield for a bit when he first came over. But he didn't come from a city. In China, I mean. So I guess he wanted to live somewhere quieter. I'm not sure.'

'And you never wanted to take the place on? It's a shame, it was in your family for years.'

'Not really my style,' Sally laughed. 'London suits me much better. And there was no way my brother wanted to run it.'

'Can't believe you didn't want to give up the bright lights. Think of the headlines, though – Michelin-starred chef comes home to open takeaway.'

'Yeah, I'm not quite a Michelin-starred chef. Not yet, anyway.'

'Okay, but you do work in a restaurant that cranks out grub that Michelin thinks is worth a star?'

'Yes. I'm the Head Chef, it's just not my restaurant.'

'And you didn't fancy running this?' I pointed out of the window as we parked outside the restaurant.

'I'm an odd one, aren't I?'

'Come on, get out the car, freak show.'

The Golden Dragon – formerly Chen's – sat on the main street through the village. What had been a nice restaurant, and along with the pub, the only eatery for a few miles, had now been split into a takeaway and an independent fried chicken place. Sal marched in quickly, not taking in the new façade at all, and immediately started speaking Cantonese to the girl behind the counter. Within the first few words, I could see the young girl becoming progressively more terrified, and after another sentence she disappeared into the back. I looked at Sal.

'What?' she said.

'What did you say to her?'

'Just passed the time of day and asked if we could order off menu or whether there were any specials. Don't think she understood a word.' A middle-aged woman appeared who nodded at Sal and began the conversation Sally had wanted to have in the first place. There seemed to be some debate, the older woman frequently gesturing to the menu behind her, and Sal, maintaining a permanent smile, but getting more and more frustrated, finally barked out a series of words that were clearly our order. The lady wrote them down in such flowing symbols it was a joy to watch her pen strokes, then she disappeared into the back. 'Just the same-old same-old stuff I'm afraid. Shame.' I looked at her, trying to read behind her eyes. 'Not the way my parents ran things.'

'Hey, it's okay, hun.' Which was one of the lamest uses of an already poor comforter, but was all I had. I put my hand on hers on the counter.

'Yeah, it is,' she said with a sad smile. 'It doesn't really bother me. Here. This place isn't me any more – the same as it isn't you. I'm just glad my folks aren't around – they'd have hated it. Always wanting to push people – challenge them. To innovate, I s'pose.'

'Is that where you get it from?'

'I dunno, he was a hard old taskmaster and we didn't get on at all in the kitchen.'

'He'd be proud of you now, though.'

'I guess. Never came to eat at a place where I worked, though, despite being invited enough times. Mum would always make excuses for him, that he was busy and stuff. He could've if he'd wanted to.'

'Was he pissed off that you weren't gonna take this place over?'

Sal, blew out her cheeks and sighed, sagging against the window. 'I don't know. We never really talked. Like, *never*. He was an old-fashioned Chinese guy I guess – kept his counsel, bossed his women folk and didn't ask anyone else their opinion because it didn't matter.'

'No wonder he fitted in so well round here.'

'Yeah.'

'Hey let's pop to the shop and get some booze before the food comes.' We marched a few doors down to the shop and bought some bottles of fizz. By the time we returned, the younger girl brought out two large white carrier bags containing a number of foil containers and some paper bags, twisted at the top.

'You didn't?' I exclaimed.

'What didn't I?'

'Order chips?'

'Yeah, girl, course! Chinese chips – gotta love 'em.'

'Can't wait to come to your restaurant.'

We jumped in the car which slowly filled with the aromas of Chinese food during the short drive back. There's that moment whenever you have takeaway food in a large group at someone's house, when suddenly there's a mad production-line of people doing things; passing plates around someone else's back, a bowl of chips lifted over someone's arms as they serve up noodles, drinks being poured, full plates being moved somewhere else while more empty ones were pulled from their warming place in the oven. And all the while people calling out their orders to make sure everyone got what they wanted.

And then silence. We sat in the front room on the giving-up-the-ghost sofas, and crunched on prawn crackers while stuffing noodles and rice as if we hadn't eaten for weeks. And as our hunger was gradually satisfied, we returned to conversation, and the matter in hand.

'So the lake tomorrow then,' Clara said with a mouthful of rice that dropped out in clumps onto her plate.

'You are one classy babe. Didn't you say you *weren't* middle-aged…?' I smiled sweetly at her.

'You know what to do, Flip. No, I was just saying that, you know, tomorrow, we have to be prepared that the lake might not meet our expectations.'

'What d'you mean.'

'It's just that we've got all these great memories of our time there, and the place might not be as we remember it.'

'Those memories are turning out to be pretty unreliable at the moment anyway.'

'She means that we should be prepared for the lake to be a shit-tip of a puddle and how the hell did we ever go there more than once,' explained Katie.

'Yep. That's what *she* means,' smiled Clara.

'You should go to the community centre and see if there are any other records around, too,' said Janey, savouring every morsel of her food.

'That might take a while – we probably won't get time tomorrow. Tuesday? Can everyone hang around that long?' I asked.

'I'm on shore leave,' mumbled Clara, her hand mercifully in front of her mouth this time.

'I can probably fudge another night off – I never take any leave so they owe me loads,' nodded Sal.

'I can work on my phone Tuesday, so I can manage,' Katie's availability just left me, and all eyes turned for my decision.

'Not got a lot of choice, have I?' I smiled back at them. 'But if I have more than a hundred missed calls tomorrow, I might have to go.'

'Sounds fair to me.'

∞ ∞ ∞

Once again, Janey started to flag as we finished the meal and we all gently made fun of her, dancing round her in the kitchen filling food waste and recycling bags, suggesting that she wasn't doing anything to help clear up. Our ten-minute tidy-up done, we quickly hugged and decided on a steady stroll back to the pub. It had rained during the evening and there was the smell of wet grass in the air, leaving a freshness I would never expect in the summer. The sky was clearing now, the moon and streetlights competing to make the spookiest shadows. We linked arms, mainly to stop Katie from swaying too much and sauntered down Stow Lane. We really did try to be quiet, but were a little too giggly and some lights in bungalow windows went on as we made our way home.

We turned right at the bottom of Stow Lane, taking a quick glance into the darkness of Lake Road where the streetlights abruptly ended to signal the village limits. It was like someone had drawn a curtain of black across the edge of civilisation. Across the road, the executive housing development that used to be Sowerby Farm was almost too well lit, with old-fashioned looking streetlights on every corner. We rounded the pond, an unbroken mirror reflecting the moon above, and headed up Cooper's Lane. The most direct route back was by cutting along the cycle track behind the old houses, but we definitely didn't want to do that in the dark. Back then we used to call it dogshit alley, and who knows what it was like now. Besides, personally, I was starting to feel a little scared of the dark. We turned for home at the end of the lane, opposite The Golden Dragon, and went by the hairdressers and the mini-market that Katie's parents had run all those years ago. Rounding the bend I could see The Wheatsheaf ahead on the left, surrounded by tall oak trees, cloaking it in shadow, with moonlight all around.

As I watched, one of the shadows moved. From the front wall of the pub, something skittered out into the middle of the road. My first thought was that it was a fox, it was low to the ground and the limbs looked slim, like an animal. And then, halfway across the road, it stood and appeared to face us. I could clearly see some sort of hat with a brim, and a jacket hanging below the waist. Paranoia gave me its opinion, but I thought it was probably just a guy who was a bit pissed and had maybe been bent over, throwing up after a heavy night. And then he spread his arms wide and started to spin around, slowly at first, but then faster and faster, throwing his head back like a figure skater, and I could swear I heard him laughing. And I was screaming, a memory from before starting to come back, of the hat, the jacket, the monster in front of us. More than a memory, a whole slew of them ram-raided my brain, crashing over dolls and cuddly toys and days at the lake with images of faceless demons and fear and death. The others held on to me, either for their own comfort or mine as the Shadow Man taunted us fifty yards away. And then he stopped. Like a dancer at the end of a routine, suddenly halting all movement, his jacket flowing round him like a cape. It seemed like he was looking directly at us for a second or two, before he ran off to the side, sprinting away along the opposite side of the pub. I started in pursuit – with no idea what I was doing or what I'd do if I caught up with him – but by the time I reached the lane beside the 'Sheaf he was gone.

Chapter 13

— Then —

Something's Out There

'Something's out there,' I said.

'What do you mean?' Katie asked.

'I saw him.'

'Who?'

'The Shadow Man.'

'Fuck off,' said Clara.

'Last night.' I said, 'in the rain.'

'Oh come on,' said Katie.

'No it's true.' I paused. 'I know it sounds crazy, but I didn't imagine it honestly.'

'Okay so what happened?'

'I was bored out of my head with it raining all day. I ended up camped in my room so my parents wouldn't give me any jobs to do.'

'Yeah, me too,' said Sally.

'After tea, Ray went out with Lisa, and Mum and Dad were watching telly. It got dark really early because it was so grey and horrible. The streetlights even came on at eight o'clock – but I love it when it rains so hard it looks like rain in a film, you know, that's obviously being sprayed from a fire engine, so I'd kept my curtains open. I kept looking up to watch it. Then I saw something on the lawn. It was weird, like a spot-the-difference quiz thing. I couldn't work it out. But then I realised there was a shadow at the edge of the trees. The streetlights are really bright and throw a lot of shadows across the garden. But then there was a new one.'

'How can you be sure? It's a big old garden,' Katie asked.

'Because it's my garden, K, and I know what it looks like. It's the view from my bedroom – I've seen it a million times. This was different.'

'What did you think it was?'

'I can't remember, but I do remember looking down at my comic again to see if it would just go away.'

'And did it?'

'When I looked up again there was this figure in the middle of the lawn, bold as you like.'

'A figure? Like what?' Clara was becoming more intrigued.

'Like a man. A guy stood on our big lawn.'

'What did he look like – what was he wearing?' Janey's interest was piqued as well.

'It was dark and he was in shadow, but it looked like he was wearing black – jacket and trousers – and he had an odd-shaped hat on, like a trilby that Madness wear.'

'What did you do?' Katie asked.

'I ran downstairs. I wanted to make sure he couldn't get in anywhere. He scared me, I just knew he was the Shadow Man. It wasn't late and still warm, so I didn't know whether Mum and Dad would've closed the windows or locked the door. I went to the back door and locked it, and checked all the windows to see if they were shut. I popped my head into the lounge and the curtains were closed. I didn't think they'd do that if the windows were still open. Then I went to the dining room – probably shouldn't have turned the lights and he might not've seen me. I could see him standing on the lawn, framed by the open window. We stared at each other – I must've been lit up pretty clearly. I ran toward the open window. But so did he.'

'Shit, he ran towards you?' Janey sat back.

'Yeah, he took two or three steps forward – speeding up, you know like you do when you're breaking into a run – like he was trying to get there before I could close the window.'

'Fuck. How close did he get?'

'I couldn't go straight there, I had to swerve round the table, and he disappeared from view. By the time I got to the window, my hands were shaking like hell and I could barely get hold of the handle. I could see him coming from the corner of my eye, getting to the edge of the lawn, jumping across the border, maybe less than ten yards away. Finally I managed to close and lock the window and I ducked to the side because he was still coming, charging at me, as if he was going to come right through the glass.'

'What did he do?' Katie asked.

'I had my back flat against the wall and he slammed into the glass at full speed – I don't know how it didn't break. And then he slammed his hands against the glass again, either in frustration or because he was trying to scare me.'

'You must've been bricking it.' Clara put her hand on my shoulder.

'I leaned forward, away from the wall, looking across and there he was, right by the window. Staring at me. Except he didn't have a face.'

'What the hell?'

'Yeah, I don't know either.'

'How close was he? To the window I mean.' Sally had been quiet but her curiosity had grown.

'Just the other side. It was really scary to be so close to him.'

'So what happened – you both just stared at each other?'

'I was frozen to the spot and I couldn't stop staring at him. He just stepped back to the lawn, stretched his arms out wide and tilted his head back, as if he were drinking in the rain. Then he slowly started to spin around, getting faster and faster, his feet stepping over each other like he was country dancing. I remember seeing water droplets flying off him where they'd collected in his clothing and on his hat. He must've been dizzy after doing it a few times but then he just stopped and stared me down again.'

'But he didn't have any eyes, right?'

'No, Sal, but he was facing me and there wasn't anything else for him to look at. He was staring at me alright.'

'Then what?'

'He just turned and ran off, out of the garden and away.'

'Where did he go?'

'I don't bloody know, Sal, I didn't go out and follow him, I was shitting myself.'

'What did you do?'

'Dad burst in wanting to know what the bloody racket was. I told him a bird must've flown into the window just as I was closing it. He could see I was shaking so he gave me a hug and didn't ask anything more. He went back to the lounge, and I must've paced around the house six or seven times, checking every single window and door over and over again, always ending in the dining room, looking out the window – half expecting him to jump out at me. I just kept doing it in a loop as if I'd gone batshit crazy.' I cleared my throat before continuing. 'So then Mum and Dad were getting ready for bed.'

'That sounds early?' interjected Clara.

'It was about ten – about right for them.'

'When I'm an adult, I'm never going to bed before midnight.'

'I had to get a drink, I was in such a state. When they were in bed I raided the drinks cabinet. I stayed up for ages, trying to calm myself down.

'Why didn't you phone?' Katie spread her arms in an exaggerated shrug.

'I dunno it felt weird, it felt odd – it still does. I thought you wouldn't believe me, I suppose. Besides it was late and I couldn't really without my parents knowing something was up. It sounds crazy, doesn't it. How is anyone gonna believe a fucked-up story like that? And there was all that stuff with Todd.'

'Yeah, it's been a fucked-up week alright,' said Katie, summarising things concisely.

'I had a phone call last night,' said Janey quietly.

'When?' I asked.

'It must've been after you saw him.'

'Okay, what happened?' I asked, already predicting in my head what she might say.

'The phone rang – I didn't take too much notice. Mum answered and next thing she's calling, saying it's for me. It was a bit odd because it was getting late – maybe ten – so the only people who might ring would be you lot and Mam would've said who it was. Anyway, I came to the phone.'

'It wasn't one of us though was it?'

'No, Sal. I answered and there was silence. Well, just what sounded like breathing.'

'Like a dirty phone call, breathing?'

'No, not really – not that I've had any of them – but not like they are on the telly anyway. It was just like someone was breathing on the other end of the phone, as you would.'

'So this didn't seem odd, that somebody rang you, didn't say anything, and obviously wasn't any of us?' I asked.

'Kind of, but I thought it was someone messing around – maybe it *was* one of you lot or one of Luke's gang who'd got my number. I was just waiting for them to make the first move. To be honest, I thought they'd just hang up.'

'But they didn't,' said Sal, never more rhetorical.

'No, they sighed.'

'They did what?' Katie pulled a face, shaking her head slightly.

'You know, a sigh. Air escaping from your mouth.'

'I know what a sigh is, Janes, it just sounds a bit weird.'

'And the funny phone call on the back of my seeing him dancing in the rain wasn't weird already?' I shook my head.

'Why do you remember him sighing?' Clara was trying to ignore our bickering and keep Janey on message.

'Because it sounded old – like air escaping from a cave or something. Like a hiss almost. It was scary, really scary, because I've never heard a noise like that.'

'Okay, so you knew it wasn't us dicking around by this point, right?' Katie asked.

'I s'pose so. Look, I'm not sure what I was thinking or feeling. All I really knew was that it was fucked up.'

'So, go on, what happened next?'

'I said *Hello* again, Flip. I was getting ready to put the phone down. I might've stayed there for ages but that sigh had kinda jolted me and made me want to get out. Then he just said 'Janey?' Which freaked me out even more.'

'Why?'

'Because it was a voice I didn't recognise saying my name, that's why.'

'What did he sound like?'

'Like it was the Earth talking, like rocks moving over each other, like something… ancient. Old and deep and scary.'

'It wasn't just someone putting a voice on. Pranking.'

'No, Sal, you've not got what I mean. It wasn't a gravelly voice. It's like saying someone can do an impression of a jet engine. Sure they can sound a bit like it, but they can't sound like the presence, and the vibration and the echoing through the sky, and that's what this sounded like. It felt like he could be talking to me through the earth without a phone.' Katie and Clara looked at each other. 'Okay, sounds nuts, but you've seen him, Flip, you know how he made you feel, you know what I mean, right.

Right?' Janey needed some affirmation, and as usual it was me she came to.

'Yeah, I know what you mean. You mean his voice surrounded you rather than being like someone talking on the phone. It was huge, like an ant describing a person's voice.'

'Yes, something like that.'

'Is that all he said?'

'No. He paused for a second, waiting for me to answer but I got scared and clammed up.'

'I wouldn't have, I'd have told the fucker to go prank someone else.'

'It wasn't a prank Clara. It's what he said next,' Janey started to cry, big bumper tears rolling down her cheeks.

'Hey, it's okay. It's alright, he's gone,' Katie put her arm round her. 'He ain't gonna get you when you're with us,' she said, with as much bravado as she could muster. 'Do you wanna tell us what he said?' Janey's head had dropped, her long straight hair forming a curtain around her face, her tears falling onto her jeans. 'Janes?'

'He said. 'I am the Shadow Man, and you will die!'' Janey took a deep breath to calm herself, but let out a large sob instead, her chest heaving. 'And when he said…' she sobbed again, 'When he said… you know the last word, it was like a screech, like the sound of brakes screeching on a train or something, like someone drawing their finger nails down a thousand blackboards.' Katie had wrapped both her arms around Janey now.

'Fuck right off,' added Clara supportively.

'What did you do?' whispered Katie.

'Put the fucking phone down on him.'

Chapter 14

— Now —

A Sort of Homecoming

It had been a particularly uncomfortable night. We'd let ourselves into The Wheatsheaf after our encounter outside and I was in no mood for a restful night's sleep. The bar was closed and only the night manager was downstairs, but thankfully our rooms were modern enough to contain mini-bars. We re-convened in my room and piled the combined beverage options from our rooms in the middle of the bed. I think I must've downed most of the vodka straight away, before slowing down somewhat. There wasn't a lot of conversation. We stared at each other, held hands, tried to control our breathing, and didn't talk at all for a while.

'So he, it, whatever the fuck we're supposed to call him is still here,' I said.

'Whatever it is, it's definitely after us,' said Sal.

'You know, when he started to spin, some things came back to me – that was what was most upsetting – memories from before –'

'Like what?'

'I don't know, King. Images. Flashes. Stuff I don't understand. Like that blank face close up as if it's on top of me. Of fire – people burning.'

'Are they are old memories coming back, or are they just…'

'What?'

'I don't fucking know – what am I, a psychologist all of a sudden? A construct. A bunch of things you've seen now that you're putting together as if it's a memory from before.'

'Bloody hell, this is how you talk after you've been drinking?' Clara asked.

'No. Memories are coming back big time. I've gotta work out where they belong and what they mean. Anyone else getting that?'

'I'm getting things coming back to me, but not as clearly as that,' said Clara and the others shook their heads.

By the time that most of the spirits had gone, it was two o'clock and we were all pretty drunk. The others drifted back to their rooms, with Sal sharing Katie's twin, and I fell asleep in my clothes on the bed. Thankfully, during the night, the Drunk Fairy appeared and undressed me, although I had no recollection of it.

∞ ∞ ∞

Abject terror combined with drinking spirits in miniature form, no matter how much you mixed them, seemed to be the perfect formula to avoid a hangover. I wouldn't say I was fresh when I awoke but I was a lot more okay than I had any right to be. After breakfast I walked over to Janey's to pick up my Discovery. I was tempted to call in but didn't feel like going over the events of last night again, so I just quietly drove away. Back at the pub, Katie was still getting ready, *why are you putting make-up on to go to the lake?* We finally climbed into the car and set off. We drove by the pond and at first glance it was unchanged from thirty years ago, but then, looking more closely it seemed… unkempt, uncared for, like nobody could be bothered any more.

It made me think, what is thirty years in the overall history of a place? I grew up here, spent my formative years here, strutted around as a teenager here because I really did feel like I owned the place, and vied for territory with a gang of boys who were doing the same.

Vied for territory with a gang of boys.

Why did that suddenly spring to mind, and why did it trigger something? My *spider sense* was tingling just thinking of it. What did it mean? Whatever, it was beyond the reach of my sub-conscious, and a new layer for another day perhaps.

This is my home village. The place I'd called home – and still did sometimes. But is it? I wondered if I could actually call it that? I'd lived there for eighteen years, sure, but in the lifespan of a village that had been around for hundreds of years, it was nothing. And that was nearly thirty years ago. After leaving home for good, I only returned periodically, for weekend visits – hardly anyone who lived here now would remember me. There'd be even fewer in another ten years. So now I'm a stranger here, as any of the residents of the new houses that had sprung up around the pond would attest if they were twitching their curtains as I stood outside a house I used to know, eyeing me warily until I moved on or drove away.

It's like I'd never existed.

No legacy here, no history, no nothing.

I was a blip in the timeline, a minor biological load and then gone. Could anyone truly regard a place as their home? Or were we all just passing through? I suppose that if generations of your family had lived somewhere, and had become entrenched within the folklore – the story of the place and the family becoming completely entwined – then maybe that could be regarded as your home.

And how long would that last when you and your kin were gone? A generation? Two?

But what if your attachment to a place was so strong, through a story, an act or an injustice, that you couldn't leave. If the bond was so indefatigable that you found a way to exist beyond your bag of watery cells, to transcend the human condition and sidestep death itself – your memory and your spirit intertwining to keep you here forever. What if that was what we were up against?

Christ, I think of some weird fucking shit when I'm driving.

The car bounced along the road, which was little more than loose chippings compressed into the surface, so typical of round here. We headed out onto the lake road.

I'd never driven out to the lake, not in all the times I'd come home to see my parents –it'd never occurred to me to go there. So I'd only ever travelled along Lake Road by bike. We sped past the bungalows on the outskirts of the village, looking slightly less immaculate, slightly more lived in, their gardens definitely more mature. The road twisted and wound, snaking its way between the fields, with the hedgerows guarding the produce held within. The once ostentatious house on the left was empty and abandoned, with broken windows and a front door hanging off the hinges. One of the two lions from the gatepost had been knocked from its perch and sat in the gateway, a sad guardian for the story of what lay inside – another short-lived act within the history of the village, and I wondered who might remember the people who'd lived there in years to come. The road to Newlands Farm, which had once been too impossibly rutted to cycle along, was now tarmac, and joined untidily with Lake Road itself. The road went straight for half a mile or so and was still framed with trees – I was pleased that an overzealous developer with a chainsaw hadn't decided to clear them away. Clothed now in their summer plumage they formed a proper avenue, so much so that it could almost lead to Hobbiton. I drove along, surprised by how much countryside remained; you'd think the developers would've been all over this place, making a massive estate of houses or something. It was all the same as before. Maybe it was a condition of getting planning permission. We reached the end of the trees and didn't find any locals with hairy feet. The road curved up and to the left, but where there had once been the farm and its outbuildings, there were crisp, precise, identical houses lined up in a row. Five of them, all painted white with black slate roofs. The right-hand fork in the road was still there but was closed off by a heavy wooden gate, with a sign hanging from it that read 'No admittance without valid fishing permit.' I suspected that those entering with a permit were few and far between because the gate was chained shut, with a heavy padlock.

'Oh shit, looks like I forgot my permit,' I said, as I reversed the car up to the gate and got out. We climbed over, Katie struggling to do so having decided to wear a short skirt today, and headed up the lane so as not to attract any further attention from the new residents. Walking along the lane was like going back in time – it was almost as we'd left it – wheel ruts, nettles and tall bushes that had become even wilder over the years, reaching out to catch us. The track wasn't completely overgrown, though, so I suspected that some type of vehicle used it, just not very often. The track mirrored the road, rising upwards, and we would've been visible to the new houses for a short while before we came to the small copse of trees and disappeared behind it. The skeleton of the rusted barn had long since collapsed to become a fossil, but the patch of nettles and brambles remained surrounding an old piece of farm machinery – *was that there before?* I couldn't remember. The track climbed again as we walked up the last fifty yards to the lake. My pulse started to race and my skin contracted to form goose pimples. The hair stood up on the back of my neck and I felt like we were being watched – not from the houses, but from the trees. We exchanged glances – I'm certain the others felt it too but I didn't want to seem pathetic by mentioning anything. We walked the last few steps to our lake. Yes, fuck it, no matter how short a time we'd spent here, in the history of the village and the lake, it was ours. It meant so much to us back then, it could surely never mean so much to anyone again.

Our lake.

The lake itself was the same. Timeless. Or so it seemed. If I could've described it for an artist to draw it would've looked like this. Sure, the distance between this side and the little peninsula was shorter than I remembered and the trees had grown up a lot – one massive silver birch almost blocked the path round the shore after the spur.

'Our tree's gone,' said Katie. And that's how we started. The big tree Janey'd attached the swing to had collapsed into the water and was just a rotting partly submerged trunk. It made me sad that such an old tree had succumbed and that our timeless lake wasn't that at all. Everything succumbs in the end. We did a full loop around the lake, seeing how the clumps of bulrushes had spread and taken over in parts, and how the undergrowth had almost cut off access to a large part of waterfront. Wildfowl still skidded to a halt and took off from the deeper water, unconcerned about us. We quickly walked around the far side, nearest the houses, hoping no one would see us and start asking questions. Finally we reached our bank by our beach on our lake. It was like a homecoming.

'Why are we here?' I asked, sitting now where I'd always sat – in my spot. 'What are we doing here?'

'I thought we'd been through this, to support Janey and to try and get to the bottom of all these memories that are coming back,' Katie replied.

'Yeah but why are we *here*, right now, at the lake, what are we doing? What's it going to achieve?'

'It might jog our memories even more, to bring even more of it back to us. This was *your* idea.'

'Yeah, I know; and it sounds wishy-washy,' I surprised myself at how harsh I was being. Too much to drink for the second night running or too little good quality sleep. 'I'm going for a walk.'

Peering through the dense bushes at the edge of the copse, I could see the entire clearing was now overgrown with fern, bramble and rooted suckers of trees, forming six-foot-tall versions of their parents. Without something to clear out the brush, there was no way anything bigger than a rabbit would be able to get through. This wouldn't be a good hiding place for us these days, not like back then when we hid from Luke Lewis and his gang.

Luke Lewis.

I walked briskly back along the bank, back to the spot where we used to leave our bikes and turned along the track, heading to the upper lake the long way round. The others fell into step behind me, finally coming round to my way of thinking that sitting staring into the middle distance was achieving nothing.

I turned left off the farm track onto the now overgrown trail that would take us the 'secret' way to the top lake, rather than following the road all the way around to the back, where quarry vehicles would've gone all those decades ago. The old fencing, which we'd pushed to one side to scramble through, was still present, although rusted and crumbling away, leaving large holes everywhere. A new chain link fence had been erected in front of it, perhaps only a year or so before, with a similarly new 'keep out' sign attached with cable ties.

'That's a new fence,' said Clara.

'So I see,' I replied, grateful that someone was stating the bleeding obvious. Immediately in front of our old gap in the fence, the new fence had been cut in a straight line up from the floor to about three feet high.

'Someone's cut the fence.'

'I can see that too,' I replied tersely.

'What?' asked Clara, arms raised horizontally out to her sides.

I bent down and pulled the two cut halves open as far as I could to squeeze under and through, swearing as I brushed my hand against the nettles that were growing right up to and through the fence. Rubbing my hand I trampled them down in the immediate vicinity, and held the fence apart. Katie muttered that she was getting too old for this, then hitched up her short denim skirt to her waist before squatting down comically like she was about to pee and duck-walking through the gap.

'Ooh, knickers. Things have moved on,' Clara smiled sweetly, which was answered with a glare as Katie adjusted her clothing. Walking up the slope from the fence, the place seemed almost how we'd left it, the trail banking wide around the lake, the water much shallower than in the other two, the unpleasant smell from the mud or the water itself. I walked over to check there wasn't something dead and rotting in it. The zinc garage had gone – removed so that no trace of it remained, leaving an even wider stretch of compacted gravel, with clumps of weeds growing up through the stones. We walked over to where a large piece of plywood board lay innocently on the ground. Rotten around the edges and weathered so it had delaminated and curled up, some parts had worn away like mice had been gnawing at it. Clara and Sal lifted one side and flipped it over, uncovering the hole that we'd expected to see, but perhaps hoped had been filled in. Without any preamble I sat on the edge and dropped down, landing on dust as if it were age itself, and being engulfed in a small cloud.

'Come down, it's okay,' I said, looking around, 'Well, as okay as it's gonna get.' We'd all come prepared this time, so we'd head-torched up and were carrying varying sizes of hand torches. Katie had a large lantern. It seems we all carried torches in our cars for emergencies, and when I was packing for the trip, I'd decided to pack my families camping headtorches in a 'just in case moment.' The drop into the main chamber was familiar but I was startled by what I saw in front of me.

'The walls are covered in blood,' Clara continued her commentary for the stupid, but I couldn't say anything this time. It was as if someone had left some cans of red paint around and then gone wild dipping their hands in and drawing on the walls. Large handprints were clearly visible at the end of long smears, like the head of a comet, there were numerous large splatter patches with droplets spraying off them, and bizarre scribbling or 'almost' drawings.

'Where's Dexter when you need him?' I asked absently.

'Anyone fancy a dip in the lower part?' asked Katie. I looked at her, then at her clothing, then back to her face again.

'What? I wasn't planning on going all Bear Grylls today, okay?'

'It's okay, I'll go,' I said, in a tone that clearly said 'if you want anything done…'

I was a little thinner the last time I did this – not much, I keep myself in shape, go to the gym, walk the dogs and get into the hills with the family when we can, but you know, approaching middle-age and all that. I sat in the gap and wiggled forward, the unyielding rock squeezing me harder than my husband ever could, my hips painfully sliding through at the last moment when I thought I might get stuck. I tried not to think about how I was going to get back out again. I dropped onto the lower step and into the wide low chamber, lit with the green glow from light filtering through the water or algae or whatever it was. Shame none of us was a biologist. In truth, my memory of the last time I was here wasn't great, but I put that down to the visibility, something that wasn't going to be a problem today. Beautiful stalagmites rose from the floor, taller than me, stalactites hanging down towards them, ready to knock the senses from the unwary. I carefully made my way around the slippery stone forms, making sure of my footing on the sloping ground. The all-terrain shoes I used for 'off-roading' back home confidently gripped the treacherous wet floor. I slowly made my way over to the darker patch on the right, peering down into the stagnant pool and seeing the same glow I had thirty years before. What was the algae that glowed and got churned up by ships' propellers that I'd seen on the TV? *Bio-something.* Would that stuff grow here in this little pool?

I stepped back, inching carefully around a stalagmite, and my breath caught in my throat as I looked up. I stifled a scream, and both my voice and my vomit caught in the back of my mouth.

'Flip! What is it? Flip are you okay?' Clara's voice was edged with worry and fear. Without answering I turned to run, colliding with the stalagmite, my knee crunching horribly against the wet rock, sending a sharp pain through my leg and a sick feeling to my stomach. Then I smashed my head into a stalactite. I saw stars, my knee gave way, and I fell, grazing my hands on the rough rock floor. For a second I was groggy, barely able to work out where I was or what was happening. The throbbing in my knee and head brought me round and I remembered what I'd seen.

'Fuck this.' I sprang to my feet and limped away as fast as I could, periodically turning back, my head torch illuminating the far wall and confirming I hadn't been seeing things.

'Flip, are you okay? Flip!' Clara sounded like she was panicking, but I couldn't speak, tears and blood were pouring down my face making me almost blind and my heart was hammering so hard in my chest that I thought it might come through. I arrived back at the hole and saw Clara's head poking through the gap, quickly replaced by hands reaching down to help me climb back up. As I was pulled onto the floor of the upper chamber, I had three pairs of eyes staring at me for an explanation.

'Jesus, Flip, what happened?' asked Katie.

'Did something hit you?'

I was too upset to speak, but I pointed back to the hole and between wracking sobs managed to get some words out. 'Go... and see... Please... some...one... go and see.' I sat with my head between my knees trying to get my breathing under control as Clara immediately wiggled through the gap, a little more easily than I had. There was a pause for what seemed like forever before we heard from her, her voice muffled by the rock, but unmistakeably her.

'You can fuck right off! Fuck me, this isn't happening. Fuck you, you fucker. Fuck!' She was next to me within a minute, shivering, her arm around my shoulders.

'Would somebody mind telling me what the fuck is down there?' asked Katie.

'There's more blood, King. Someone's written in blood down there,' offered Clara.

'Written? What's it say?' asked Sal.

'It says, 'I'm watching, Flip.''

∞ ∞ ∞

Now we'd been there a few days, Janey's felt like the nerve centre of the operation, even though we weren't staying there, so on our return we simply burst through the side door into the kitchen. I'd recovered somewhat but was still shaken and was looking forward to some sweet tea.

'Hi,' Janey's head popped around the kitchen door from the hallway, 'Be right there – I've made cakes.' Now that I'd sat down there was indeed the tell-tale smell of baking in the kitchen and a hugely appealing chocolate cake sat cooling on a wire rack.

'Not just a pretty face then,' said Katie eliciting a wince from the rest of us as, at that moment, Janey bustled in and immediately shooed Sal away from tea-making duties.

'If I'm not out in the field with you, the least I can do is feed and water you,' she smiled happily, turning to us. 'What? What's wrong? What's happened?' Janey's smile slowly became a frown as she looked at each of us, finally dropping her eyes to mine as I'd plopped down at the table.

'Oh my God, Flip, what happened? Are you okay? Let me get the first aid kit.' I realised I probably looked a mess, covered in blood, dust, cave mud and quite possibly some snot and puke. Sally filled Janey in with the details as I sat staring into space, allowing her to bathe the worst off my face.

'Jesus, Flip. I'm not sure what to say,' she said uncharacteristically, squeezing out a cotton wool ball in warm water enriched with Milton. *No doubt used for cleaning her prosthesis.* She dabbed away at the last of the blood on the cut on my head. 'This could probably do with a stitch.'

'No way,' I said. 'Have you got any steristrips?'

'Yeah. Hang on. I can't believe what was written down there.'

'It's what it means more than anything else,' I replied. 'What does he want?'

'He's trying to communicate,' said Sal.

'Or take the piss. Or scare the shit out of us,' said Clara.

'Mission-fucking-accomplished, I'd say.' Sal flopped down next to me.

'If he takes notice of us, knows our names, then we aren't faceless, nameless victims. He either thinks of us as adversaries, or isn't interested in getting us,' said Janey.

'That's a bit of a leap isn't it?' said Katie.

'Think about it. How many other people have had their name inscribed anywhere?'

'Who the hell knows? He might have done it for others who went down there over the years.'

'He?' Are we making him real now?' asked Clara.

'He, it, whatever. What I'm saying is, this might've been a regular occurrence for people who visited that place,' said Katie.

'Yes, true, but I bet we're the only people who've gone there of their own free will,' said Janey, missing the irony of being the one who hadn't gone anywhere.

'And not been taken there for whatever reason,' said Clara.

'Exactly.'

'I've just remembered about Luke Lewis,' I said, my still shaky hands now cupping a mug of hot tea and Janey cutting me a slice of warm cake. 'I'd never have expected you to get into baking.'

'I'm amazed I fit it all in, what with work, the garden, the Rambler's Association…' Janey winked her one eye. 'I've been doing it for years – practice makes perfect.'

'*Bake Off?*'

'Only if Hollywood comes here,' Janey winked again.

'You could bake in your polytunnel.'

'What about Luke?' asked Sal, standing by the worktop holding a small plate and spooning a chunk of sponge into her mouth.

'He was taken to that cave.'

'Well, you're surmising that's what happened.'

'No, he was, I remember. I remember seeing him there.'

'Fuck off – seeing him, how?' asked Clara.

'I dunno, I've just got one image of him kneeling on the ground outside the cave, it's at night because it's dark, but there's some light coming from somewhere – maybe a fire,' I said.

'Wow, good knowledge,' said Janey, topping people up with tea. 'Anything else?'

'Nah, it just came to me after coming out of the cave and smelling the lake and the bank. I nearly puked again and this image came back.'

'So it was worthwhile going there after all?' asked Katie.

'Yeah, I suppose it was,' I nodded, standing corrected. 'Wish I hadn't gone down into the lower cavern though.'

Chapter 15

– Then –

Laurendon Show

The Laurendon & District Agricultural Show was one of the highlights of the year. So little went on in our group of villages that the annual tractor parade generated much excitement. It didn't have the same magic as when the Fair came to town at the end of the summer – that was always a bit different. The lads who worked the rides always seemed romantically 'other' to us, their big, heavily tanned arms tightening the bars of the waltzers just a bit too much on us excitable girls, making us giggle and dream of running off with them and the Fair. The Show was definitely different.

We'd stand on the corner of Stow Road the evening before, watching the parade of tractors. Some genuine classics – or at least they looked that way to the untrained eye – that were obviously well cared for, painted in bright orange or yellow, with chrome polished until it was shiny, travelling from show to show to give tractor nerds a hard-on. Some years you even got an old traction engine that would rumble along Hadley Road. The rest were old shit-heaps that had been rusting behind a derelict barn for most of the year before being painted in garish shades of blue or green to chug, fart and otherwise pollute the air along the main road to gate-crash the party, before turning into the showground ready for people to wander past the next day. Of course they didn't actually pollute the air, because pollution hadn't been invented back then.

Our parents all knew that we wanted to go to the show, but used to make us do jobs beforehand under the threat of not being allowed to go. So I'd gone shopping to town with mine, Janey had to mow the lawn, Clara had to take their elderly pooch for a walk which she *never* had to do, but at least it was before the times when you had to pick up after your dog and you could let it shit wherever it liked.

I called Janey. The dial on our avocado phone whirred and clicked its way around as I called her number.

'481?' Janey's mum always answered with the last three digits of her number, like a lot of older folk. When phones had first come to the village, there were only three numbers, but with growing numbers of people and interlinked telecommunication, a prefix of eight-seven-one was now added to Laurendon numbers, and even a national dialling code, so you could phone places as exotic as Stockport or Margate.

'Hi Mrs Pullman, is Janey there, please?' I waited while her mum went off to get her, and after an age of my mum looking at me and pointing at the clock on the wall, just to remind me of who was paying for this local call on the cheapest rate at the weekend, Janey came on.

'I've just finished cutting the bloody lawn. When do you want to go?'

'I've just got back from town, so give me half an hour?'

'Okay. You heard from the others?'

'No. I'll call them and let you know if there's anything different. See you at the showground.' If only we could've posted our movements on Facebook so everyone knew, rather than having to make individual phone calls.

You knew the show was in full swing when you could hear the sound of the PA system echoing out over the village. The words were unintelligible background noise that, in the end, you filtered out like the sound of your washing machine or car engine. The announcer probably worked at a train station, spouting similarly unintelligible information about delayed trains and which platforms they were no longer coming to.

We finally met outside the show at midday, the sun beating down from the cloudless skies, already teasing the mercury higher. We'd all dressed for the summer in shorts and strappy tops, meaning we'd look as red as lobsters later. On entering the field, you were always presented with portable showrooms for double glazing, car dealers and agricultural manufacturers. Each had a range of sales promotional materials, like brochures, stickers and fliers. We would take a plastic bag from a place offering such goodie bags and proceed to fill them with as many brochures as possible. It wasn't really a competition, but it was – you hadn't 'done' the show properly if you hadn't collected the brochures. The entire village was full of nerds. The first part of the show always felt sparse, and when you'd got past seeing giant brand-new green tractors or reversible ploughs, there wasn't much left to see. All the exhibits and entertainments were gathered around the perimeter of the field, leaving a series of show rings in the centre. The largest of these was for the equestrian competition and exhibitors in the heavy horse, hunter and pony classes, with progressively smaller rings for cattle, sheep and even fancy rabbits. The main ring was demarcated by blue rope – which looked suspiciously like bailer twine – periodically tied off on a series of rusting metal posts, with an open section for competitors to access the ring. The smaller rings were essentially corrals of straw bales, arranged two or three high depending on the jumping capability of the competitors, with smaller pens off them, where animals would wait their turn to perform – like a farming equivalent of a Formula One pit lane made entirely of straw. From above, the show rings would've looked like an irregular cross-section of a beehive.

Ed Grissholm, one of the oldest farmers in the village, stood inside one of these corrals, surrounded by sheep with curling horns. The Joint General Secretary of Laurendon Agricultural Society was dressed in green wellington boots, tweed trousers pulled up so high we called them chest warmers, and brown braces over a white checked shirt. He looked every inch the farmer, and even on a day like today, wearing his best clothes, he still stank of cow shit. His ancient battered trilby was pushed back on his forehead, revealing a patch of skin that was crying out for some protection in a red glowing protest, and his jowly three-day growth of beard and red countenance, made him look permanently angry.

We walked around the top end of the show, passing another loudspeaker affixed to a freestanding pole, which itself was drowned out by the unmistakable sound – and petrol smell – of a generator powering the world's worst bouncy castle. We'd navigated our way past the myriads of new car salesman, outdoor gear and riding tack stalls. Now from the far end, we were faced with the engine-room of the show. To our left, just beyond the bouncy castle, was a marquee full of exhibits in categories such as 'Best jam and other preserves,' 'Largest onion,' and 'Carrot that looks most like a dick.' It's possible I made the last one up, but you get the idea. There were plenty of cake prizes, and bottles of homemade wine and beer, so at least some of the judges would be enjoying themselves before they moved on to the flower arranging.

We passed Mr Grissholm, tending his sheep, and stopped to admire them, leaning over the bales to encourage the fairly tame animals to have their ears rubbed. Bo Peep he was not.

'I've seen you lot, riding around,' he said, his angry eyes surveying us like Mr Potato Head.

'I'm sorry, Mr Gruesome – have we done something wrong?' I asked.

'You young buggers are all'us up to nah good.'

'Can we pat your sheep, please?' I asked, really quite scared by this seemingly mean old fart.

'Aye go on then. But be careful of 'em. Don't get 'em excited or they'll never have a chance.'

'Fucking old codger,' said Janey when he turned his back again, and several of us pulled faces at him. We petted the sheep rather half-heartedly, then Sally mentioned ice cream and we all got up to leave. I immediately felt faint, and would've fallen if Clara hadn't grabbed my arm. A haze started to close in on my vision and the aperture of clarity shrank rapidly, seeming to disappear in the distance.

'Hey are you okay? Flip?' Sally said, giving me a shake, holding me up by my shoulders. The dizziness receded but all I could do was nod dumbly. 'Let's get you a seat.' We moved away from the show rings, not wanting to further irk the farmer by sitting on the straw bales. They led me to the vintage tractor display and I plonked myself down on the running boards of an old Fordson Major. I put my head in my hands, breathing heavily and heard someone say. 'Let's get her a drink.'

'I'll go,' came the reply, from Janey who ran off to find a drinks stall.

I don't know if I was dehydrated, or if it was the strong smell of the animals on such a hot day, or maybe the sweet smell of hot dog stalls mixing with candy floss, but whatever it was, the sickly faint feeling gradually faded and I sat upright. In the distance I could see Janey returning carrying a small cardboard box. She grinned as she approached and handed me a red 'cup' drink, the ridged plastic container nestling in my hand as I plunged the straw through the foil lid and took a long drink of the horribly synthetic raspberry flavoured juice. Janey handed out various coloured drinks to the others, and then delved back into the box to bring out Fab lollies. As she looked down, pandemonium struck behind her. My head had just stopped swimming but it was still in the showers trying to pull its bathers off when I looked up. Janey was in focus, but behind her was a blurred yellow glow. I blinked several times and screams drew the attention of the others who turned to look. With a final blink my eyes cleared and I saw Ed Grissholm, standing in his straw corral, surrounded by his sheep and consumed by fire. His body and face almost unrecognisable behind the flames. He stood, arms outstretched as panicking animals tried to jump the two-layer straw barrier to escape, a relatively easy jump for calm sheep, but almost impossible in their desperation as they fought to get away from the burning farmer, who was twirling around and setting fire to more of the tinder-dry bales. Before long the whole lot was burning and the smell of roasting mutton was as strong in the air as that of roasted human. I could hear a high-pitched whine, like the propeller engine of a small plane or the sound of air escaping from a tightly-squeezed balloon neck, and I realised it was Mr Grissholm himself, keening a cry of unimaginable pain, despair and fear. Through the flames I watched his flesh seem to melt away and he ceased to be Mr Ed Grissholm – the grumpy bastard farmer who never liked us riding along the public paths across his land, but who really wasn't such a bad person – and he became a thing, a thing whose left leg melted away and caused him to collapse down on that side, arms waving as his screams died. Numerous people from other exhibits and stalls trained fire extinguishers on the corral, but the straw was too well-alight. Ironically, a planned demonstration by the fire service had been cancelled because they were short-staffed, so there was precious little anyone could do to put him out.

'Oh Jesus, how did that happen?'

'You must've just walked past it, Janey,' I said.

'Yeah I can't believe I didn't see anything – he seemed okay when I went by – or maybe I didn't take too much notice?'

'A man's dead here, you can't just say you didn't notice,' snapped Clara.

'Look, I'm sorry, Miss-fucking-Marple, but I wasn't going around expecting someone to burst into flames, okay?'

'Hey it's okay, Janey, there was nothing you could've done even if you were right there, was there? You might've got horribly burned yourself,' I said.

'Christ, it's awful and we're just standing watching the freak show. Let's go shall we...?' Janey gestured with her head.

Fab lollies and multi-coloured cup drinks in tow we wandered back to the top of the showground to make our way to the exit. The sheep corral was only now being extinguished with the hose set up to fill the animal water troughs. The pumped pressure was so poor, however, all the men might've stood around and pissed on it and been just as effective. In the middle of the straw, now largely turned to ash, was a grotesque tableau of man and sheep, with an impossible arrangement of blackened bodies and limbs, all steaming under the limp water spray. Grown-ups tried to shield little kids from seeing the nightmare and for the first time that day, tannoy-man had shut-up. We moved a little quicker when we heard the approaching sirens, and left the field just as two police cars and a fire engine turned in.

'Did you see his face melt?' asked Janey.

'Bloody hell and his leg just burned away and snapped.'

'Fire's gotta be bloody hot to take bone with it – look at crematoriums.' We all looked at Janey, who was the brightest amongst us but sometimes her knowledge, as in this case, bordered on the macabre. 'What?' she asked, shrugging her shoulders.

In the days to come, the fire service concluded that Mr Grissholm's cigarette end had come into contact with fuel slowly leaking from the bouncy castle's generator. The whole area, they reckoned, had been drenched in accelerant. An accident waiting to happen. After that the show was never really the same. It was ultimately cancelled a few years later as bigger and better regional shows took over from those in local villages. It was the beginning of the end for Laurendon in more ways than one.

A week later, we stared into the flames of the fire we'd built down at the lake and discussed what had happened. 'That wasn't some leaky petrol and a cigarette.' I said, purely to put it out there, and waited for the disagreement.

'He would have to have been soaked in the stuff – he went up like a match,' agreed Sal.

'Something else is going on,' Janey said, tossing a couple of branches on to keep the fire going. 'I didn't smell petrol when I walked past.'

'Oh fuck off, the lot of you,' said Clara in typical fashion. 'What else is going on? Go on.'

'We just walk past a guy, don't smell anything, don't see him smoking, and yet five minutes later he goes up like tinder from petrol and cigarettes,' I said.

'So why would they lie, and what really happened?'

'Well, the Shadow Man is what,' said Janey. 'It has to be him.'

'In the day? In front of all those people?' asked Katie.

'Maybe he's escalating, maybe he's doing it to show us how he can get at us.'

'And you don't think that the official explanation has any merit?' asked Clara.

'No. Not really. So yeah, I'm ready to believe that the more plausible story is a vengeful two-hundred-odd-year-old spirit.'

'Janey –'

'Fuck off?'

'Well, I wasn't going to say exactly that, but yeah, why not?'

'If there was something plausible, something reasonable, even something that was someone's fault, they'd have found it out and released it, but they haven't. If they could come up with something else, something believable for those that were there, then they would've – but they haven't. Their story's shite. Even spontaneous human combustion would be a better story than what they've come up with, but they can't use that *again* can they?'

'I dunno, I get the historic story but I'm still not quite believing the Shadow Man as here and now,' said Clara, her face a picture of doubt and confusion.

'Give me a better scenario. None of us believe the official one. So what else is there? And what if, when you take away the most logical of explanations, you're left with something crazy.'

'That's called something isn't it?' asked Sal.

'Yeah, fucking scary.'

Chapter 16

— Then —

You Reap What You Sow

For all the days that we went to the lake, or cycled around, or visited people that summer, there were plenty of other days when I, and we as a group, were just bored. Today was like that. I knew a couple of the others were busy so we didn't have anything planned. I called for Janey but she wasn't around. It did nark me a bit that no one had asked me to tag along with whatever they were doing, but we weren't each other's keepers, and if they had things to do then it couldn't be helped. I was mindlessly riding around, thinking of something to do – not wanting to go back home because Mum would've loved to have had a little slave for the day, or might perhaps have decided we should do some baking together, which would've been excruciating. I rode around the pond and into the new estate of bungalows, climbing up the tall kerbs and jumping off, trying to get both wheels to land simultaneously and imagining myself on some trials bike, jumping over cars or something. We did that sometimes. Not jumping over cars, of course, but building ramps and racing along seeing how far and how high we could jump. With today's mobile video technology we would've no doubt been embarrassed at how poor our efforts were, but back then we jumped high and far, often being sent flying when we landed.

I rode through the village and saw Luke Lewis and some of his mates outside the shop, which had been my planned destination, for an Ice Pop before heading slowly home. I was on the bend that swept into the car park, about to turn in, but on seeing them I immediately swerved down dogshit alley, the lane that would take me behind the housing estate opposite. I stopped and looked over the fence panel bordering the garden of the first house, standing on my pedals and pulling myself up so I could peer over the top of the panel. The unplaned timber dug into my hands and the sweet-acrid smell of new creosote stuck in my nostrils. I could see the boys outside the shop, dicking around as usual, riding their bikes at each other and making a game of pushing someone else to the floor. Luke looked up after his own mock joust. His friend, whom I didn't know, rolled on the floor clutching his shin where Luke's pedal had scraped him. Luke seemed to look straight at me, although I was sure I was hidden behind the fence. He seemed to stare for a long time, then looked away again. I wasn't going to hang around and wanted to put as much distance between them and me as I could. I pedalled hard along the narrow lane, sometimes riding over tarmac, sometimes mud. When they'd been laying the road to the new estate, they'd sometimes poured leftovers onto this lane and badly flattened it down. I slalomed around the copious quantities of dog shit as I went, watching fences and brick walls flash in front of my eyes before wrenching the bike back onto the middle of the track. If I'd met anyone coming the other way I'd have been finished – at this speed there was no way to avoid a collision. After half a mile of constantly looking over my shoulder to see if I was being pursued, I burst out of the lane across the pavement and bounced down the kerb onto the road, seeing the car too late as it sped along Cooper's Lane, bearing down on me, my pace making a quick change of direction impossible. I wrenched the handlebars and leaned down, dropping my knee as if I was riding in Moto GP. The driver slammed on the brakes, the tyres screeching and white smoke spewing from the rubber. All four wheels locked up – ABS being a luxury for the few back then rather than a standard feature. I was winning my battle with my bike, leaning over at almost a forty-five degree angle, my own tyres complaining almost as much as the car's. Turning with almost oil-tanker slowness, the bike gradually came round, now missing the front grille, now the front wheel, but the car wasn't stopping. With the brakes locked, it skidded along the tarmac, closing the distance, the skid causing it to drift toward me with the camber on the road. I had a split-second decision to make – brakes or power – and in that moment there was only one option, and that was power. I pedalled hard, the tyres screaming as they tried to grip the road, the angle of the bike meaning that there was so little traction and the back wheel started to slip from under me. Dropping the bike would've been game over – I would've gone straight under the car's front wheel – but I'd committed to this and had run out of options. I eased my pressure on the pedals slightly, yet the drift continued, the wheel gliding in slow motion, but only for an instant before the tyre gripped. Finally being pushed in the right direction I started to come out of the lean and shot forward, my hand reaching up to push me clear of the passenger wing mirror as I straightened up and flew past the skidding car. The driver angrily sounded his horn again and again as he reached a halt in a cloud of smoke. I could hear him shouting and swearing even as I cycled away. For a second I wondered if he might turn around and come after me, and once again I was on edge as the adrenalin spiked, heart thumping high in my chest, the blood pounding in my ears.

I headed along Cooper's Lane, flying by the entrance to the bungalow estate and the short cut to Janey's, gradually allowing the bike to slow until I rode lazily around the pond as my body calmed down. My thoughts were elsewhere and I found myself out on Lake Road – I'd never been out here by myself before and it felt odd to be here without the others. I had no idea what I was going to do – go to the lake I supposed – but I didn't have a plan and was going with whatever happened.

I'll never know why I looked over my shoulder – I suppose you do from time to time when you're cycling, but there was no engine noise or anything to alert me. I just did. Luke Lewis was coming up hard behind me, his face contorted with anger and hatred, sweat staining the front of his t-shirt. He was closing the fifty-yard distance between us like I was standing still and once again I had to act fast. In that moment I thought I saw another bike way behind us on the road, but I could've been mistaken – I hoped it wasn't another of his friends. I stood on my pedals, pushing down and almost liking the feel of the massive strain I was suddenly putting through my thigh muscles, feeling them scream in protest, but knowing they needed to give me everything. Of all the things that my parents would save money on, would skimp on, my bike wasn't one. Kids' bikes back then weren't massively expensive road or mountain bikes, but mine, which would probably be called a mountain bike or hybrid today, was light and fast. Despite my putting my foot down, Luke was still closing quickly and I looked back in time to see his powerful arm swinging at me in a big arc to try and knock me off. I ducked, my forehead almost hitting the handlebars, and veered across the road aiming for the entrance to the tiny track that led to the first lake – much smaller than 'ours' and far too close to the road for us to frequent, but it was the best option to get away from the open road where he was going to be quicker. I heard him swear somewhere behind me as he had to rapidly change direction to give chase, then I was enveloped by the trees, disappearing from view and gaining a few yards. I realised I'd only ridden this path a couple of times and I desperately searched my memory for any reconnaissance advice. Branches had overgrown the path as it swept down to the water, scratching and clawing at my face and arms as I flew along, my legs pumping for all they were worth. I heard him on the path behind, my advantage shrinking as he closed the distance between us on his bigger bike. The lake appeared on the left and I contemplated jumping in, backing my own strong swimming ability against his, but I realised that I would be trapped in the water, particularly if more of his friends turned up, and I'd be a goner. The bank slowly rose up above the waterline and I left the path to ride along the top of it, goading him to follow me off the path which took a wider route around. The surface was uneven and slightly muddy, my tyres struggling to maintain a grip. In front of me I saw another trail leading off at a right angle to the one circling the lake, leading away into the woods. I wrenched my handlebars hard around, once again throwing myself into a precarious lean to swing the bike over and make the turn. The back-end started to slide out, speedway-style before the tyres gripped and I shot down the side of the bank and along the path, cutting right in front of Luke who had stayed on the perimeter, going the longer way round but maintaining more speed. He was racing so fast that he missed the turn, but sadly failed to mangle himself in the bushes just beyond. I heard him curse again as he stopped to turn his bike, and now I'd put some genuine daylight between us as the path undulated up and down, turning left and right, rising to the wooden footbridge over the feeder stream to the lake, the bike almost airborne as the path dropped down again on the other side. My lead over him had only lasted a quarter of a mile and he was right behind me again. I needed to do something to shake him off and quickly as my legs tired, my muscles burning, my breathing more laboured. Like a popping cork, I burst from the trees onto a farm road, not as rutted as the one leading to the second lake, but running in a parallel direction several fields over, further out from the farmstead. My pace slowed on the uneven surface, baked hard from the sun, and I almost fell a couple of times. There were gateways to fields, some harvested, some not, and I hoped that I might find someone on a combine or pulling a baler who would provide me with a haven. Round bales stood like standing stones in the fields. I daren't look back but I knew he must be close, and I hoped he was having more difficulty than me on the terrain. The next opening on the right was a wheat field and I turned into it, trying to do something to throw him off and gain some time. I immediately realised my mistake, as the field had yet to be cut, the wheat heads catching around my legs and slowing me almost to a halt as I tried in vain to pedal against the tide.

And then he hit me, jumping from his bike to grab me around the waist in a rugby tackle, and dragging me to the floor, my foot catching painfully against the pedals as I was pulled clear. He landed on top of me, knocking the wind out of my chest. I struck my head against the hard ground, being given no cushioning by the straw we were flattening around us. For a second I saw stars and as my senses returned I found myself flat on my back, pinned underneath him.

'I've got you now, you bitch,' he sneered down at me, saliva dribbling from his mouth. He pinned my arms above my head, bringing our faces together. 'I'm gonna enjoy this.' He licked my cheek and I could smell him. I wanted him to smell of stale sweat and piss and bad breath, but he smelled of almonds and sandalwood and Aquafresh – *why did I think of that?* His free hand came up under my t-shirt and squeezed my breasts, trying and failing to get underneath the underwired front of my bra to my flesh beneath. I wanted him to be fat, sweaty and ugly, but he wasn't. He could've been a nice boy in a different life, one that all the girls wanted, as opposed to just the rough ones that hung around him like he was a trophy, keen to be the next one to suck him off. I wriggled as much as I could, trying to bring a knee up to shove into his groin and bucking my hips to try and throw him off.

'That's it, you enjoy yourself – I know I will.' His face was twisted into a leer, his square-jawed good looks now almost monstrous, like he was evil itself. He reached down and fiddled with his clothing until he could shove his jeans down, freeing my hands for a moment. I took the chance to reach up to his face with the intention of taking out his eyeballs or tearing his skin so badly that I could get away. He saw me coming, swinging his big arm round and slapping me hard across the face, making my jaw feel like it had dislocated and knocking my head sideways. My vision fogged over for a second once more and as I came to, he'd taken hold of my hand and brought it down between us, between his legs, to where his erection stood, awaiting orders.

'Be nice, bitch,' he ordered, raising his hand again as a threat as to what might happen if I wasn't. He held my hand against him and started to rub against me. I felt the bile rise in my throat and almost choked on the taste, bucking forward in a retching spasm. Suddenly I was on my front, his strong hands flipping me over, and I knew I was in even more trouble now because I had fewer options to fight back. I tried to prop myself up on my elbows to turn over or to get onto all fours, but he just pushed me back down, his knees either side of my hips, holding me in place. He folded my arms behind me and tucked the bottom of my t-shirt up over them, pinning them as he went to work on the waistband of my shorts, dragging them down, taking my underwear with them and I felt the warm sun on my exposed bottom, as the rough straw scratched my belly underneath. I felt his cock resting against me and knew that I was running both out of ideas and time. I was screaming at him, shouting and swearing, calling him the worst things I could think of, making as much noise as I could to try and put him off or attract someone's attention. His hands were all over me, roughly poking and prodding at my most intimate parts. I heard him spit on his hand and felt him move his hips, knowing exactly what he was doing. He grabbed hold of my hips and I tensed, holding my breath, terrified, wishing the ground would just open up and swallow me, wishing my heart would just stop, thinking of my parents, my friends, thinking of anything that would take me away from here and now. There was a noise off to my left and movement on top of me, for a split second the weight increased and I tensed even more waiting for something to happen, and then he was gone, his knee digging painfully into my bottom as he rolled off, giving a surprised cry as he did so and almost rolling me over before his hands released. There was a scuffle off to the right and I looked across, through the wheat, which had now been further flattened. Luke had been hit from the side by a figure dressed completely in black, and he was pinned underneath it now, like he was trapped by his own shadow. The figure had no face, it was just a black void, and wore a black-brimmed hat.

'What the fuck, get off me or I'm gonna fuck you up!' Luke screamed into the Shadow Man's void, and in response it screamed back – not a shout or a cry but the wailing screech of metal on metal, or a dentist's drill. And it was ear-splitting. I saw a fumbling between them and suddenly Luke let out his own cry of surprise and extreme pain as the Shadow Man must've twisted his still-exposed manhood or something. I didn't hang around any longer to watch, I got up and ran, pulling my shorts up as I went. My bike looked okay and it wasn't in a tangle with Luke's so I managed to pick it up as I ran. I was almost out of the field when I paused. I'd been brought up with manners, and it didn't matter what that thing was, it had saved me.

'Er. Thank you,' I called back. The Shadow Man looked like he was devouring Luke, his head moving backwards and forwards over his face like some shark rasping away at a whale carcass. The wailing and screeching noises it was making were terrifying. Hearing my voice the creature looked up. Well, no it didn't.

It? I can't think of it as a he. The creature? Just what the fuck is it?

It can't have looked up because it didn't have a face, but it raised its head anyway and seemed to be looking or sensing in my direction. For a split second I wondered if I'd made a terrible mistake. If the Shadow Man had only intended to separate us to deal with one at a time, and now it had been alerted to my escape.

Jesus how stupid could I have been.

After another second it bent back to whatever unspeakable thing it was doing to Luke.

Now I fled. Jumping on my bike and flying back along the path at a frightening pace, barely able to hold on to the handlebars and trying to block out thoughts of pursuit by faceless, black-clad, two-hundred-year-old wraiths. For the second time that day I almost broad-sided a car as I joined Lake Road – not even looking as I shot from the farm road out onto the tarmac, delighted to have a proper road surface under my rubber grips. The driver sounded his horn angrily and swerved away from me, shaking his fist, but I didn't care. Better to die under the wheels of a car in Normal-Land than at the hands of a would-be rapist and an apparition in the Hammer Horror film I'd just left. I looked at my watch – how long had I been out there? It felt like a long time and I was shivering with cold even in the heat of the day.

Just over an hour.

Shit, it felt like longer than that – it wouldn't even be lunchtime yet. I asked my legs for one more effort to get me home, surprising Mum when I walked into the kitchen.

'Is everything okay, love?'

'Yeah, why?'

'You look a bit… rattled.' She frowned slightly.

I'll say.

'You sure nothing's happened this morning?'

Well, it's like this…

'No, fine. Well. We did go up and down the hill a bit and my legs are exhausted – it got a bit competitive. Katie, you know. So I told the others I was heading home. Might just take it easy this afternoon.' Mum frowned again. 'That is unless you need me to do anything?' I realised in trying to be normal I was being the least normal that I'd ever been.

'No love, you take it easy. Just as long as everything's fine.' Mum walked off toward the lounge, throwing me the occasional backwards glance.

∞ ∞ ∞

'Shit a fucking brick!' said Clara in surprise.

'So you saw the Shadow Man?' It was less of a question from Katie, more a statement. I'd spent the last fifteen minutes giving them the warts-and-all story.

'Yeah, again.'

'And he just came out of nowhere? In daylight?' Janey was fascinated.

'One minute Luke Lewis was there, on top of me, about to… well, y'know. The next, bam, he's been knocked off sideways and this figure, all in black, is on top of *him*.'

We were lazing in my back garden, Mum having delivered squash and biscuits, and a couple of cans of Top Deck lemonade shandy. I'd spent a few hours in my room reliving what had happened at the lake, dissecting every moment, being scared, looking out of the window to see if he might be there. He being the Shadow Man, not Luke Lewis, whom I thought was probably in a whole world of pain by now. Or worse. Time wasn't making things go away so I called the others, and by mid-afternoon we had Jammy Dodgers on a tartan rug.

'So when you left, the Shadow Man was all over him?' Katie asked.

'Yeah, Christ knows what he was doing.'

'Was he… hurting him?'

'I don't know – the scream he let out, right in Luke's face, the sound of it. That was just as scary as everything that Luke had done and what I thought he might do.'

'What did it sound like?' asked Janey, intrigued.

'It was like a wail, but it wasn't how it sounded. It just sounded… old.'

'What does *that* mean?' shrugged Katie.

'Like there was hundreds of years of anger or badness stored up inside of him and he was letting it out.'

'So you think he'll kill him?' asked Clara.

'Shady's not known for his ballroom dancing, is he?' said Katie.

'Hang on a minute, if Luke dies, will it be my fault?'

'What?' asked Katie, incredulous.

'Fuck off,' said Clara.

'In what bizarre fucked up way is Luke 'the rapist' Lewis' potential death, remotely your fault?' Katie's eyebrows were approaching her hairline.

'I dunno,' I said, knowing I sounded very confused. 'I just wonder if I'd have stayed there, maybe I could have got the Shadow Man off him.'

'Listen to yourself, Flip,' said Janey. 'When he appeared, you were worrying that the Shadow Man might go for both of you, that he was just attacking because he came across you, not that he was doing it to protect or defend you.'

'And he still might have done. I can't believe you fucking said *thank you*,' said Sally.

'Maybe he really wasn't trying to protect you. Maybe he took out Luke, and you were going to be next,' said Katie.

'So why'd he let me go then?'

'I dunno but he certainly had his hands full at the time with Luke, didn't he? If he goes after you he loses Luke. He might as well stay as he is – one kill's better than nothing.' Katie shrugged.

'Don't say that, 'one kill's better than nothing', bloody hell.'

'I can't believe what we're talking about.' Sally was shaking her head.

'Yeah and that kill is better that way round than it being you.' Katie sounded like she was trying to end the debate.

'I want you to listen to me, Flip,' said Janey staring intently at me. 'Luke was about to force himself on you. And who knows what he might have done afterwards. We might never have seen you again. So I think, in that field, it was you or him. End of. The Shadow Man appearing just meant it went in your favour.'

'But he could be there, alive. He could be somewhere and someone could still help him.'

'Haven't you heard what I've just said? That boy could've raped and killed you. And you're thinking of setting up some kind of search party? You reap what you sow.'

'But he's only a young lad. What if he could change, what if he's messed up, what if he just needs help?'

'Wasn't him that needed help earlier today, it was you.' Janey said definitively. 'And let's be honest, even if you did phone the police, and say 'oh by the way, I was being attacked by somebody, and guess what came to my rescue. Think the cops are really going to take that seriously?'

'So we just leave him to die, or whatever?'

'Janey's right,' said Katie. 'Not your problem, and not your call – there isn't anything you or we can do.'

'We can go looking for him.'

'Oh yeah, 'cos the few of us are gonna stand a chance against that. Just how do you propose to fight it? Hairspray and zit cream?' Katie put the brakes on the Mystery Machine.

'There's no harm in going back out there – just to have a look – it'd be like going to the lake like we normally do.'

'I'm creeped out,' said Sally.

'Flip, this is crazy. If he doesn't come home and he does turn out to be missing, then you can tell the police that he chased you because there's been bad feeling, that you rode round the lakes and lost him then came home and haven't seen him since. That would work and it's not technically lying either.' Janey seemed pleased with the story she'd created.

'So we never go to the lake again? We never let that happen with Luke's gang, and I'm not gonna let it happen now. I'm going back tomorrow. Anyone else in?'

'Oh for fuck's sake, Flip… Yes I'm in.' Clara shrugged, looking at Sal.

'Well of course we're all in, but I still think it's a bad idea,' said Katie, speaking on the record for everyone.

Chapter 17

— Then —

Harsh Language

We met at Janey's the next morning and shared the contents of our backpacks. It was like a collection of tools for a bad DIY show – I had a monkey wrench, Katie a crowbar, Sally a hammer and a Stanley knife, and Janey had nothing.

'What are you gonna fight him with, harsh language?' asked Katie.

'I never thought about taking a weapon.' Janey looked between us, then seemed to have an epiphany and disappeared into the garage. We could hear muffled sounds of clanking metal, as if tools were being moved around so she could choose one in particular. She re-emerged a few minutes later with a big smile on her face.

'All sorted?' asked Sally.

'All sorted,' Janey replied enigmatically.

'Very mysterious,' Sally smiled as she shouldered her pack and picked up her bike.

Like a sheriff and his posse, we saddled up and rode out in search of bad guys. 'We need a plan,' said Janey as she snaked along Lake Road.

'I think we should retrace Flip's steps from yesterday,' said Katie. 'We should go out by the first lake, around the paths and out to the field where Luke caught her.'

'Yeah, if we come back the same way Flip did as well,' said Sally, buying into the thought process, 'we'll have covered every bit of ground. Let's hope we find something.'

'Agreed then,' said Janey. 'But that isn't quite what I meant. I meant we need a plan in case we see the Shadow Man.'

'My plan,' Clara offered, 'is to shit myself and then run like fuck.'

'We don't know what this thing is,' said Sally. 'It's certainly not a man, because the man was burnt at the stake two hundred years ago. So, whether it's a spirit or some pure evil energy or whatever, a few garden tools aren't gonna touch it. There's no way to fight it.'

'So why did you come then if you didn't think we could do anything?' I asked.

'To be with you guys. And because I'm fed up with watching *Why Don't You?* on the telly.'

'We're gonna have to try and talk to it aren't we,' I said. 'See if it can be reasoned with, to find out what it wants.'

'We don't know if we can communicate with it – we don't even know if it'll speak,' said Katie.

'We don't even know that it'll recognise us in the same sort of plane to be able to communicate,' said Clara.

'Jesus Christ. I don't understand a word of this stuff.' Sally shrugged.

'It did respond when I said thank you, though. It might understand us, or it might understand that we are trying to communicate with it, even if it doesn't understand or communicate back.'

'It certainly responded to the stupidest thing anyone has ever said to it,' said Katie.

'But it didn't piss itself laughing, so maybe it doesn't understand us,' added Clara.

'You don't think this thing could be... alien do you?' asked Sally.

'Really? Jesus, Sal, we're not hunting for a spaceship you know. You're reading too many trashy books,' said Katie.

'Oh, because that's such a crazy fucking notion and the idea of a two-hundred-year-old ghost or evil spirit or whatever, is so much more believable. At least if it wasn't from Earth it might explain how long it lives and maybe resists fire...? Oh fuck – this is going so far away from what I can understand it's crazy.'

We turned off the road just before the first lake, going through the tiny gap in the trees at a much more sensible pace than I had yesterday. I half expected to see Luke floating face down in the lake, the Shadow Man doing his 'spinning around' dance on the far bank.

The lake was empty and still. A kingfisher skimmed the top of the water making small ripples, looking for fish beneath the surface. Moorhens and coots floated serenely in the shallows whilst a mallard loudly admonished them as only a big-mouthed duck can, thoroughly spoiling the tranquillity of the scene. Our arrival caused a flurry of avian activity on the near bank, with waterfowl flapping across the surface to put some distance between themselves and the bizarre interlopers. We circled around the lake on the path, not climbing up the banking as I had done, cycling slowly and keeping our wits about us. We were all shit-scared then. Partly because of what we might find – like parts of Luke hanging from the trees or a pile of ashes with his shoes by the side of them or something, and partly because at any moment, going past any tree, we expected it to jump out at us. But that fear gave us an edge, it made us feel alive. I looked at the others and saw a maturity beyond their years, a seriousness – a drive to get to the bottom of this, and to do it together.

'I can't believe we're fucking doing this,' said Clara, succinctly summing up everyone's feelings.

'There's nothing here by the lake, let's go out to the field,' I said.

'How did you get there?'

'The path up here on the right, Janey.'

'You been to this lake much before then, Flip?' asked Sal, being the first one to turn onto the narrow, overgrown track.

'Only once I think – we came up here once, didn't we? Might even have been the first time we came out here, before finding the second lake. When was that, end of the second year, maybe?'

'Yeah I remember, vaguely.'

'I didn't particularly choose to come this way, I just happened to see the path and I took it out of instinct I suppose. It could've been a dead end and I would've been in real trouble.'

We rode at a much more sedate pace than on my last visit. It seemed incredible that I'd managed to stay on my bike when I was going so quickly – no wonder I was so covered in scratches and bruises, regardless of the fight I'd had with Luke. I was continually scanning the trees and bushes and clearings and streams beyond for anything; movement, a shadow or figure, wildlife scattering, anything that might lead us somewhere. We were forced to snake along in single file, up and over the bridge across the stream and back down the other side until we eventually emerged onto the farm road. It was here that I stopped.

'Everything alright, Flip?' asked Katie, sounding concerned.

How could I answer that? How could I say, *no I don't think anything'll be alright ever again. I feel like my guts are being wrenched out of me and that any moment my legs are going to go.* How do you say that to your friends when you're fifteen and full of bravado and balls? 'Yeah, I'm just a bit… nervous I s'pose. I'm not sure I want to ride my bike along this bit, you know, in case he's here. Or it's here. Or both.'

'Okay,' Katie replied in her best shop-steward tone, and turned to the others. 'Everybody off.'

We pushed our bikes along the track, past the first few gateways that I remembered noticing the previous day, and spied the more overgrown opening to 'my' field.

'There, just up ahead,' I nodded. We leant our bikes on the open gate and walked through into the waist high wheat. The edge of the field had only been sporadically seeded, which is why I hadn't noticed the crop from the track yesterday, at least not until it was too late. After the first few steps, we were surrounded by a sea of undulating wheat heads, flowing in the breeze, moving and sounding like waves. The wind whispering unintelligible secrets as it raced around and between us. I trailed both hands through the crop, feeling the hard, dry husks scratching at my skin, grounding this surreal experience to a degree. I turned to my left and just five yards away was the place where all the straw had been flattened down, the size of two bathtubs side-by-side. It was where Luke and I originally fought. I waded through the field and into the flattened area, looking for anything that might have been left behind. The others stood around the perimeter. A further five yards or so on again was another impression, where Luke and the Shadow Man had come to rest, leaving a strange pattern of broken and partially flattened straw where they'd tumbled over and over. But there was nothing else of note in the field.

'Nothing here then,' said Sal.

'I can't see any blood,' said Katie.

'Oh fuck off,' said Clara. 'This is weird and arse-puckering enough as it is without making like you're on some cop show, that there's 'no blood.''

'What did we expect though, really? A blood trail saying 'follow me'? Torn bits of clothing, leading us from this field to that and to God knows where? You only get clues like that in *Scooby Doo*,' Janey reasoned.

'You are Velma, though,' said Clara.

'What now?' Janey asked me.

'I dunno. Let's go to the lake.'

We retraced my route along the farm track to Lake Road. We looked in the hedgerows and the ditches for any evidence of what I'd described, in case anything had been thrown, discarded or left by accident. Just as Janey surmised, however, there were no clues to be found.

The short bike ride and walk up to our lake was as familiar as it was welcome. Never had two journeys seemed so different. Yet it felt strange. As if our special place had become tainted by the events of yesterday. It should feel like coming home, but it didn't. Like years later when coming home for the first time after going to university – as though home wasn't home anymore, like it had moved on. It didn't have the same sense of comfort for me anymore, it felt colder and I was a stranger. We sat in silence on our bank, staring into the middle distance, like old men in the pub. Janey lay on her back staring at the sky, watching the vapour trails of aeroplanes flying high above. The wildfowl on our lake knew us well. We'd fed them scraps of our packed lunches all summer and they'd got quite tame in the process. We recognised some from previous years – there was a Mandarin duck with very specific red and blue colouring – but others could've been one-off visitors that got lucky with the free buffet.

'Fuck! Something just touched me!' Janey sprang up, shaking her head, her hands running wildly through her hair like she was trying to dislodge some ants. 'I felt something touch me, on my head. Fuck. Fuck. Fuck. It was him, *him*, it must've been him! He's in the bushes.' Janey pointed a finger into the foliage behind where she'd been laying as she continued to dance around.

'Calm down, Janey, I'm sure there's an explanation – maybe it was an insect, or a branch pressing against you,' I reasoned.

'It was the flat of someone's hand, like if they were going to pat you on the head. I think he was going to grab my hair and pull me in, drag me off into the undergrowth. Fuck, I'm itching all over, my skin's crawling.'

I peered through the leaves into the shaded clearing, seeing no one. I pushed through the branches, adding more scratches to the list.

'Hey, don't go in there. Haven't you heard a word I've said?'

'Look, I'm not sure what it was, Janey, but we're all here together, and if it was who you think it was, let's go take a look, eh?'

'Hang on, Flip, I'm coming too.' Katie tucked her baggy t-shirt into her shorts as she came towards the tree-line, and I watched her from the other side. She emerged through the branches into the gloom, we looked at each other and the bravado we'd had in front of Janey had evaporated. Katie's eyes were out on stalks, so I knew she was as scared as me. The temperature was much lower than in the sun, and our fear made us colder again. Shadows from the undergrowth and fallen trees were long and eerie. As far as we were concerned, each one could've contained something terrifying. We exchanged glances and slowly made our way across the small wooded area, thinking of how safe it had felt just weeks before when Luke and his gang had come to look for us. I stumbled, my foot catching against something soft and I almost tripped over. I looked down and it was a pile of leaves in front of a small tree trunk. Sighing with relief I resumed my walk across to the far side, moving sideways like a crab in a crouched position, as if this would prevent the enemy from noticing me if they were watching. We combed back and forth across the woods and found nothing. We even went out and up onto the upper path that lead to the top lake, but didn't go as far as that.

Janey was disappointed on our return. 'I didn't make it up – I know what I felt.'

'You couldn't have drifted off to sleep and –'

'Dreamt it? Really? Something touched me on the top of my head. It was a hand, but like long fingered, and... cold. Like it was dead or something. There's only one thing it could've been.'

'Fair enough, Janes, but we've got nothing for you.' For a second Janey looked like she might explode at the slightest suggestion that the lack of proof might mean something else entirely, but she relented.

'Thanks for going though, both of you. It was a stupid thing to do!'

'Let's go home,' Clara echoed the sentiment that everyone was feeling. The lake might yet feel like our special place again, but it didn't now, and hanging around was the last thing anyone wanted to do.

As we cycled away, I thought about Luke Lewis, the would-be rapist who'd had the biggest surprise of all yesterday. I pictured him as the attractive young man that he was, could smell his deodorant and his toothpaste, and tried to block out the picture of his hate-filled face pressed right up against mine as he pinned me down. We'd come down here today to try and find him, or find some clues as to what might have happened to him. And we were returning empty handed.

The Shadow Man had him now.

Chapter 18

— Then —

The Big Fire

'What time will you be back, Mum?' I asked, a corn on the cob obscuring my mouth and covering my face in butter.

'Isn't it supposed to be the grown-up asking the teenager that and not the other way around?' My mum had a smile that could light up a town. She'd tied a scarf over her newly permed hair. She looked nice.

'Sor-ry!' I tried to sound surly and failed miserably. 'Nah, was just curious if it was going to be a late one.'

'Blimey, Philippa, it's a meeting about the school and about how to keep people safe after the disappearances this summer.'

'What disappearances?'

'Pardon? Don't you know?'

'No. Well, Janey did mention something about kids being reported missing after not getting home when they should've.'

'Children have gone missing, Philippa. I'm amazed you haven't heard anything, the amount of riding around you do.'

Yeah and I know one of them. 'We don't really talk to anyone, though – although it makes a bit more sense as we've had some quite funny looks from folks in the last week or so.'

'It's only because there's such a good number of you that I don't worry. I don't want you riding round on your own, and certainly don't want you out at that lake by yourself. Understand?'

'Yes mum.' *Is it okay that I wasn't there by myself but I was with a psycho from my year trying to rape me, and a two hundred-year-old dead child killer?*

There was a knock on the door, and Mum answered it to Janey's mum – smoking a cigarette as usual, something that my mum strongly disapproved of. She'd only agreed to go in the Pullmans' car because it was just 'up the road'. Any further would've made Mum choke.

'Ready, Eveline?' Janey's mum asked.

'Yes, Cynthia.' Mum grabbed a light jacket from the rack. 'Be good you, Dad'll be home soon.'

'Thanks Mum. Have a good time.'

Dad was watching *Tales of the Unexpected* having got back from work later than usual. In a dry summer, all the water company's engineers were under pressure to ensure that leaks were kept to a minimum, but they all knew they were fighting a losing battle. He wasn't in a foul mood, but you could tell he was tired and was struggling to make small-talk. It was usually better in those situations to leave him alone, and thankfully Ray was out with Lisa, so he wouldn't wind Dad up. A fire engine raced by on the main road, sirens blazing, immediately followed by another and another. Further away across the village came the sound of more sirens, which we could hear when Dad switched off the telly. We ran outside, down to the front gate and looked down the street toward the village. At the foot of the hill, about a mile away, was a huge plume of thick smoke, illuminated from below by the orange and white street lights.

'Get in the car,' Dad said quietly. He was already reversing out of the driveway as I lifted my feet in and started to close the door, and in a second we were screeching down the road. Dad threw the car hard to the right over the mini-roundabout and along Park Terrace – the rows of posh new semi-detached houses on one side and older bungalows opposite. Opposite the old school dad span the wheel and the car's rear-end was thrown out as he turned to the left, his hand lifting heavily on the brake to force the car round, tyres squealing their protest – I'd never seen him drive like that. Quickly into gear again and we roared up the hill to the new school and village hall. We didn't get very far. Another two hundred yards and there was a barrier across the road and a policeman who stopped us.

'You can't go any further sir,' said the copper after we'd climbed out of the car.

'My wife's in there.' Dad pleaded. Looking beyond the cordon, the growing crowd of gawking onlookers, the police and the firemen putting on breathing apparatus, I looked at the yellow flames rising high into the air, sparks and embers rising higher still and being enveloped by the billowing clouds of smoke.

'Then she's in good hands – we'll have her out in a jiffy.' The policeman turned to someone else who was trying to walk nearer to the school buildings. Suddenly I found my upper arm being gripped so hard I thought it might break, and Dad pushed me sideways. We went straight into the adjacent garden and deep into the shrub-border where he guided me over the low wall into next door. We ran across the lawn commando style, crouching low and concealed in shadows, then once again climbed over the wall, repeating the same manoeuvre over their wall and continuing into each subsequent garden. The image of Burt Lancaster in *The Swimmer* came to mind. Here we were garden-hopping to rescue Mum. We cleared the final wall bordering the school lane and immediately ran through the gates and round to the side of the pre-fab classrooms. To our right, two ambulances, three fire engines, an emergency tender and two police cars were blocking the whole street. We rounded the main school building, both of us sprinting flat out, and it occurred to me that I'd never seen Dad running. We emerged onto the main playground, a connecting gate the only thing keeping us from the village hall, but here we ground to a halt. The building was engulfed in flames, rising up from the windows, racing up the wooden fascias to the eaves and up above the roof, reaching some thirty feet into the air.

The old village hall hadn't been replaced like the school but been modernised to, over time, 1985 standards. The old wooden sash windows hadn't been changed, and there was no double glazing throughout the draughty, musty building. The main hall was where we'd done Christmas concerts as kids and they still held public events in there – the kind that usually had a break mid-way through to sell you tea and biscuits in that traditional 'church hall' ribbed avocado china teacup and saucer. Behind the hall, where that night's meeting had been held, was the small library and records room where Mum worked, along with a couple of offices. Despite all the old wood and church tradition, the back offices were more modern with suspended ceilings and strip-lighting. To comply with fire regulations, they'd had to turn a couple of doors into fire exits, but it came out later that there was so much crap stored in the building, that they were treated more like additional cupboards and had blocked everyone's escape.

The smoke clouds above were bright orange, lit up by the flames below. Even from fifty yards away, the heat was incredible. A criss-cross of hoses overlapped in the car park of the hall and a dozen or more firemen were either spraying water on the flames or escorting people from the building.

Thank God, some people are alive.

'Stay close, and never let go of this,' Dad said, holding up our clasped hands. It was one of the most affectionate things he ever said to me and different to the often distant and aloof parent I knew. Perhaps he just didn't know how to communicate when not in work. Or perhaps he just didn't really understand life outside. He worked too much.

We set off at a run, aiming for the turnstile gates, the heat increasing and stinging our faces. Smouldering debris rained down on us and dark ashes fell like snow. We hit the gates at a run and barely avoided getting ourselves trapped in the rotating metal arms, fighting our way through them and into the grounds of the burning building. Firemen looked across as we stood in open-mouthed astonishment at the building in front of us as it started to collapse.

'You'd better get back, mister,' said the nearest fireman. 'This whole place is going to go.'

'Is everyone out?' Dad asked, pleading.

'Can't help you there, I'm afraid. Everyone is mustering in the front car park.'

'Yes of course.' Squeezing my hand tighter still, both of us terrified that the worst might have happened, we rushed around to the front and saw hundreds of people milling around. Some lay on stretchers receiving oxygen from ambulance-men, others were bent over coughing and spluttering, smoke rising from their jackets. One couple seemed completely unaffected and stood talking, while other uninjured folks were overcome with relief and were crying. Mum wasn't at the front of the crowd, so we both scanned through the rows, trying to peer through people, craning our necks left and right to see if we could see her. Dad and I started to gently push through the survivors, needing to see her, needing reassurance. We were almost through to the other side of the crowd, with the growing and terrible realisation that she wasn't there, when the last few people parted and Mum stood before us. We engulfed her in our arms and all cried together, relieved that she was okay. Mrs Pullman stood next to her, a sooty graze on her face being tended to by someone in an overall.

'What happened?' asked Dad.

'I don't know. We were in the meeting, and Geoff Thornton was going on – you know, like he does – when I started to smell something… off. Then it became obvious that it was smoke, and we could see it coming under the doors that lead off to the library and offices. So we got out.'

'And that was it? How did Cynthia get injured?' Dad asked.

'There were flames everywhere in the foyer – the fire had really taken hold and the ceiling tiles were starting to fall in – God knows what they're made of but they were like gooey marshmallows falling on us. One of them hit Cynthia in the face.'

'Ouch,' I said. Dad went to speak to a fireman – someone in dress uniform and not overalls, so maybe the guy in charge. 'Did everyone get out okay?' I asked when he came back.

'They're not sure. Not everyone is accounted for, but they're still walking people out.'

'Oh God, I hope everyone's okay. How did it start?'

'They don't know anything yet, but the fire seems to have started in the library and records area.'

'How can they tell that, Dad?'

'I'm not sure myself, but I think it would probably be where the fire was at its fiercest, you know, did the most damage. He said it went up through the ceiling of the room and caught hold of the old wooden rafters, spreading it across the whole roof, burning the lath and plaster ceiling of the main hall and melting the tiles of the other rooms. That's how Cynthia got hurt. The chap said it'll take a day or two before they know for sure what caused it.'

'Any ideas, Mum?'

'No, we were in the back office for a while before the meeting started and there was nothing then – everything seemed fine, like it always does. Then we were in the meeting, started to smell smoke and the next minute we're stood out here.'

'Why did it take so long to get everyone out – why didn't you all just leave when you smelled smoke?' I asked.

'Because the front doors were locked and nobody could find a key. Geoff had to go back to the office to look for his jacket and ended up crawling through the smoke to get it. Everyone was panicking and hammering on the doors, pushing against each other and wouldn't let him through even when he had the keys. By the time he got back there the fire brigade were knocking down the door.'

'Why the hell did he lock the doors?' Dad said, incredulous.

'He said he didn't – he never does. And people were coming backwards and forwards through the evening before the meeting started so I believe him. I think we got locked in when we were all together in the hall.'

'When the meeting had started?' Dad asked.

'Yes.'

'Somebody deliberately locked you in?'

'I think so, yes.'

The local news and papers were full of the fire for the next few days, and there was some fire brigade spokesman on the telly all the time saying that there was no news yet. On the third day they released a statement. It said that the fire started in the records room, and it looked like it was started deliberately. There was no mention of the locked doors. They said they found the remains of a cigarette-butt in there and that may have been the cause. Then the whispers started, almost like the wind in the wheat.

Janey's mum smokes, and she smokes at work.

Mrs Pullman had the press camped on her door that week, but Mum helped to diffuse things by telling everyone that while she'd had a smoke in the car on the way up, she hadn't had another cigarette that night. Mum didn't mention about the locked doors either. It was as if nobody wanted to make public that there was an arsonist in the village who had deliberately tried to kill fifty people, as if by not mentioning it, it wouldn't have happened, and they would go away. The pressure eased on Mrs Pullman, but I knew that suspicions would still be there for a long time afterwards.

It turned out that some of the historic records of the village and surrounding areas were lost, the seemingly less vital stuff that wasn't births deaths and marriages. Only some aspects remained. Some had made it onto microfiche, and some copies had been retained more centrally, but a lot of the history of the village was gone. This didn't raise any suspicion in anyone apart from us.

∞ ∞ ∞

'It's him,' Janey said as she drank some mushroom tea. We were sitting at the lake the day after the fire, and two days after we'd been searching for Luke. It seemed odd to return, like going back to a relative's house that you haven't visited for a while – everything was there and as it should be but just something... I couldn't put my finger on it. We'd all brought towels and costumes – as if swimming was an option, just not in the buff – but no one suggested going in, which was unheard of. We were mellowing with the tea, however, and I was starting to relax, realising that I'd been on edge since we'd first turned onto the lake road.

'We can't really say that can we?' Katie replied, sipping her tea and still wincing at the taste.

'Yeah we can, he locked the bloody doors for God's sake. That Geoff said he didn't lock them and they weren't locked when their meeting started – it can only be him. He's pointed the finger at Mum, and thank God for your mum, Flip, otherwise she might be in clink right now,' said Janey.

'If it's not him, we've got two arsonist nutters running around,' said Clara.

'I don't know why they didn't say anything about the locked doors in the paper.' Janey shrugged.

'Maybe they don't want to worry people,' said Sal.

'Half the fucking village was either at that meeting or knows someone who was, and I would imagine they were all quite worried.'

'But why? What's he playing at?'

'He's coming after us. Targeting our parents – who knows what he might do next.'

'He's targeted them but there's nobody else is there?'

'What do you mean?' Sal frowned at Katie's comment.

'I mean all this stuff about other kids that've gone missing, apart from Luke. There isn't anyone is there?'

'Not that I know of,' said Janey.

'It's just the rumour-mill isn't it? People are shit-scared and so if their kid is even the slightest bit late home, they start phoning around and the news is they're missing. Doesn't matter that they've already turned up at home by the time that gets out.' Clara shrugged, as if we were helpless in all this.

'So we haven't got a lot of choice then, have we?' I said.

'What do you mean?' Janey's eyes were wide, probably from being a bit stoned, but also with a degree of excitement.

'We've gotta fight back.'

'And how do you propose we do that?' Clara wasn't drinking any tea, she was shivering slightly despite the warmth of the sun.

'I know,' said Janey. 'It's obvious.'

'Go on.' Clara had her arms wrapped around her knees to keep warm.

'We give him what he wants.'

'Which is?'

'Us.'

Chapter 19

— Then —

In Search of the Shadow Man

Both figuratively and literally the dust settled regarding the fire. The press drifted away and the report that was published later just read like a fudge. Life in Laurendon seemed to return to normal. As normal as it could be, I suppose, considering how crazy the summer had been, but nobody seemed to be trying to link anything together. The police had conducted house to house enquires the day after Luke's disappearance when we were at the lakes, retracing my steps. They were appealing for information and had apparently talked to all his friends, but nobody knew anything about where he was.

They finally caught up with me, with all of us, the day after the fire. While his parents were making appeals about the disappearance of their son – I read an interview with them in the paper where they talked about what a lovely boy he was and how he had so many friends who were 'heartbroken' that he was missing – I told the police about the Luke I knew. The bully, the leader of a gang that had chased us down Brewery Hill that had resulted in an accident that had cut his face open. The boy who's hatred for us had grown even more and had brought him out to the lake to try and find us and fuck me up. I decided against telling them about Luke attacking me and what happened then – I sensed they believed me, that they appreciated a balanced view of the boy rather than the rose-tinted one they were getting from his parents. They asked me if I thought he could be hiding out somewhere or if he'd run away from home and I told them I didn't know him well enough to say. By all of us saying the same thing to the police, I heard they went to talk to his friends again, and maybe they had to change their story about him.

We kept getting lectures from various parents about being careful when we were out and about, but because we were the only people who really knew what was happening in the village, we probably felt safer than anyone.

The next day – the third after Luke disappeared – we decided to go up to the lake to watch the sun go down. The holidays were nearly over with the end of August in sight. It had been overcast with some light drizzle in the morning – the first rain we'd had in what seemed like ages, the last time being when I'd seen the Shadow Man dance on my front lawn in the downpour. Today, when the drizzle finally stopped, the air smelled of ozone and summer storms. By mid-afternoon, however, the sky had cleared and the sun was poking through, the heat rising once again. We cycled around collecting one another, formulating our plan. We told our parents we were all going round to Katie's to watch videos. She lived in a big house on one of the new estates, round the corner from us. Her folks owned the small supermarket in the village, so we could always rent anything we liked. Katie told her parents that she'd been invited over to mine for food and we were going to listen to music together afterwards. And despite what had been going on, our parents were happy with our arrangements and didn't check – they knew we'd be safe because we'd told them. These were not the days of setting up a parents Facebook group to track our activity. It was 1985, and it was fine.

By seven we were heading out on Lake Road, and had made camp by half past, the sun hanging low on the horizon. We'd all brought supplies in small bags but Janey had a huge mysterious looking rucksack on her back. We rode out along the road, not really concerned about having lights to guide us home later.

By the time we'd had a quick dip it was after eight and the sun was starting to fade. Janey produced sticks, tinder and matches from her bag. She quickly built a wigwam of kindling over her tinder and lit it with a match, the small fire taking immediately, sparks roaring upwards into the darkening sky. We piled on some logs we'd found at the edge of the treeline before it had got properly dark, and saved some more for when those died down, the flames roaring as the fire grew hotter. We sat around and felt cosy even as the night air came down with a chill. Janey also produced Ray's stove from our storage behind the treeline and started to heat some bottled water in one of his camping pans. Good old Ray.

As the water boiled on the stove, we passed the snacks around but Janey went tramping off round the camp site, torch in hand, looking for something. Ten minutes later she arrived back, on cue as the water in the pan boiled. She sat and busied herself with her Swiss Army knife in the torchlight, adding things to the pan, before boiling it again.

'Come over here you lot,' she called a few minutes later. We'd been staring at the sunset, lost in our own thoughts of the metaphysical, having long since stopped wondering what Janey was up to. We sat around her in a circle, and she passed us some plastic cups full of mushroom tea.

'I'm still not sure I'm getting a lot out of this stuff, you know,' said Clara with each suspicious sip.

'Apart from an increasing dislike of mushrooms,' added Katie.

'Yes. That.'

It took a while for us all to drain our cups and flop back on the grass to stare at the sky, the edges of which were fading to black as night started to envelope our hemisphere. The sun slowly dropped to the horizon in a shimmering heat haze, beyond the lake, beyond the farm buildings and fields. It finally became a ball of red fire and disappeared, the sky above us turning from yellow, to orange and then red, and I could see stars poking through the fire. I've no idea how long I lay there – probably only a couple of minutes – before the fungi started to work on me. Everything above me slowly started to rotate, the sky spinning on my axis, the pinpricks of starlight moving around me. The yellow, orange and reds began to move and flow, like flames in a fire – merging and twisting, rolling and fighting together, like colourful lovers entwining across the cosmos. The sky was turning faster now and I began to feel a little sick with the motion of the stars blurring as they raced around the periphery of my vision. The flames chased each other round and the centre of rotation collapsed on itself becoming a vortex, sucking in the surrounding stars, pulling the last beams of light from them before they disappeared. Then I was being drawn in, the entire galaxy above lifting me toward the gravity vortex, drawing me to the same fate as the stars.

'Let's go swimming!' Janey cried, and her shadowy figure sprinted from somewhere behind me to create a loud splash in the lagoon. I sat up, the spell broken, or at least in part, as everything was still spinning around, despite my shaking my head to clear my senses. We all followed Janey, and, ignoring any common sense or warnings that our brains might otherwise flag up, we too jumped into the cool water. We swam silently, enjoying the almost complete stillness of our surroundings. Janey led, and we rounded the point, our senses shocked by the chill of the deeper water into regaining at least a little clarity. My lazy breaststroke was keeping pace with Janey in front as I dreamily enjoyed my surroundings becoming mild hallucinations, when suddenly she screamed. Not a cry of being in trouble or for help, but a blood-curdling scream, that must've echoed all the way back to the village. She screamed again and pointed to the shore, incapable of speaking. Finally she found her voice.

'Look at the fucking shore, it's him, it's *him*. It's the fucking Shadow Man!' I followed the direction of her finger and saw a dark shape on the shore, receding as I stared. Janey was off, kicking out hard to reach the bank, gliding round the point and leaping out of the water as soon as she felt the lagoon shelf beneath her.

'Janey, no!' I called after her, struggling to keep pace with her and emerging a few seconds behind her, the others not far behind. Janey had found her torch and was crashing through the undergrowth ahead of us, already beyond the treeline when I caught up with her. 'Janey, stop.' I could be quite insistent when I wanted to – nothing's changed since. I led her back out of the trees onto the bank where the others were shivering in the now chilly air, the warmth of the day having disappeared with the sun.

'I saw him, he was on the bank.'

'You were off your tits on 'shrooms, love, that's what you were,' Katie had picked up her towel, now damp from the evening dew.

'I'm not, I saw him, I'm telling you.'

'Janey –'

'I fucking saw him, alright?' Janey shrugged my arm off and marched off to where she'd seen the Shadow Man. 'See? Look. Footprints.' She shone her torch down onto the grass and mud on the other side of the peninsula.

'We've all been over here during the day, Janey, walking around.' I tried to be gentle and measured.

'And which one of us has got size twelve fucking feet then?' She pointed the beam of light at the large bootprints in the wet grass.

It wasn't the chill of the night making us shiver. We huddled around Ray's camping stove as Janey boiled the kettle for more mushroom tea, throwing the last branches onto the dying fire. Katie passed the vodka around. I took a long glug, the alcohol burning the back of my throat, almost making me choke, but I swallowed both the spirit and the cough reflex. The booze went right to my head, like the first hit of a cigarette or your first line of cocaine – or so I'm told. I'd drunk my fair share over the summer but this was particularly affecting me and I swayed backwards and blinked a few times, trying to collect my thoughts.

'That's it, girl,' smiled Katie, 'Get it down yer.' She took the bottle back from me, and, a more seasoned drinker, glugged a couple of mouthfuls down before passing to Clara. I felt all warm inside now and my heart seemed not to be racing as much. The kettle boiled and Janey carefully poured the steaming water over the mushrooms in her flask.

'So are we going after him, then?' she asked.

'What?' Clara seemed less than convinced.

'We said just yesterday that what he wanted was us. So let's go to him.'

'Now? Tonight? A bit pissed and a bit stoned?' asked Sal.

'You've had some vodka to warm you up and some mushroom tea to mellow you after a big shock. It's hardly like you're staggering around or anything.'

'Are you in a fit state to fight that thing?' exclaimed Clara.

'If it comes down to fighting, we're fucked. We just need to be calm, that's all.'

'Not too strong on the mushrooms then, eh?' I said.

'No, just a couple in there. Will keep our heads clear.' Janey passed around the little lid of her thermos flask which was doubling as a cup and we all sipped the steaming, sweet, earthy brew. Janey had now taken to adding sugar to the tea after we'd all complained about the taste.

'Christ this is sweet, Janes,' said Katie, pulling a face.

'There's no pleasing some people. First it's too 'mushroomy', then it's 'dogshit' – nice by the way – then it's too sweet. You are a picky lot.'

'Just wanted to have some teeth left after tonight.'

'Fussy cow.'

Just like Janey said, the heady mix of tea and vodka gave us Dutch courage and we broke camp, packing up our belongings and putting on our packs. Janey said she'd seen the figure disappear into the shadows of the copse, so we followed, knowing almost certainly where he was going. We stumbled through the brambles and gnarled tree roots, swearing more than Clara on a bad day. It seemed to take an age, but finally we started to clamber up the bank at the far end, pulling ourselves up using exposed roots and fallen branches, getting the occasional boost up the bum from behind. We reached the narrow path, emerging into stippled moonlight. In the dark, the path seemed narrower than in the day, with a bottomless drop-off on the right that a few hours earlier would've looked like a slide down a bank – almost fun on some days. There was a steady passing of the vodka bottle in one direction, and flask in the other. I didn't know what it was; the drink, the mushrooms, the adrenaline or a combination, but I was starting to feel both dizzy and sleepy – waking from my stupor as I stumbled on the path. All conversation had stopped, where it had been loud and boisterous when we started on up the track. As if in a dream, we reached the top, where there was the hole in the fence to get to the upper lake. I was swaying like I was really drunk, but feeling like I might fall asleep. Clara stumbled into me and laid her head on my shoulder, sagging against me. Janey pushed through the gap and shone the torch for us, helping Katie through, who nearly fell face first into the nettles.

'I don't feel too good,' said Sal and leaned over to puke into the bushes, Janey having to catch her from tipping all the way over. She retched a couple of times, Janey holding her hair back before she stood upright again, strings of snot and puke dangling from her mouth and nose. She wiped her face with the back of her hand. 'I feel like shit,' she said, and her legs buckled so Janey had to catch her to stop her falling. Katie wasn't fairing much better, she and I helped each other along with Clara grabbing hold of us so we staggered together.

'What the fuck is wrong?' I asked, head swimming, barely able to keep a coherent thought, and vaguely aware that I was slurring my words. We managed to get as far as the gravel area in front of the workshop, to the side of the cave, and all slowly sank to our knees. The dizziness took me over and the periphery of my vision faded to grey. The last thing I remember as I slumped to my side on the ground was Janey standing over me, a strange expression on her face. Now, remembering that look for the first time in thirty years it's obvious what it was.

∞ ∞ ∞

I'd stayed at The Wheatsheaf for too long. The lumpy bed, the seventies décor, it just wasn't like being home with Spock and the kids. No, it was time to leave. Today had to be the last day of this trip for me. After breakfast, the plan was for Katie and me to go to the community centre to try and find anything from the old records that might provide a further history for the Shadow Man. Clara and Sal were going to Janey's to hunt around on the web to see if they could flesh out the story even more. After multiple coffees and uninspiring cereal – my arteries couldn't cope with another cooked breakfast – I stood rinsing my toothbrush in a trickle of water, wondering if this trip had achieved anything. And then I remembered seeing the figure twirling round in the road the other night.

Just what the hell was going on in this place?

I answered the knock at the door. It was Clara, looking a little green about the gills.

'Are you okay, love?' I asked, ushering her into my room to sit on the bouncy castle mattress.

'No. Fucking full-grease has sat right there,' she held her hand over her upper abdomen. 'It won't make it's bloody mind up whether it's gonna go down or come back up.'

'Okay, do you want a lie down or something?'

'Oh no, Christ. Makes me want to spew just thinking about it. No, I reckon I could do with some air, blow the cobwebs off. The walk over to Janey's will do me some good.'

'Okay, we'll meet you back at hers later when we've finished up?'

'Yeah good idea. I'll tell Sal. See you later.' Clara got up to leave and we clasped hands affectionately for a brief second before she went downstairs. Katie and I had always been the obvious leaders and most out-going of the group, but I'd always felt closest to Clara. It seemed incredible to me that we hadn't kept in touch. I grabbed my keys and bag and collected Katie on the way down to the car.

Following the fire, the village hall had been rebuilt as a modern community centre, offering childcare, a full library service, multifunction rooms for aerobics classes, religious groups and meetings. Gone was the musty, damp church-hall feel of the old place. Gone was the wooden cladding and seating that had turned the old building into a death trap and had brought the roof down. For years afterwards there was debate and argument about whether the old building should be restored or not. In the end, as always, it came down to money. The community council argued that whilst the council sat around pulling its dick about historic buildings, the area was crying out for a meeting place, and of course, they could build a shiny new one that easily complied with all the fire regulations for a fraction of the cost. Hence the new centre was built and opened after I'd left Laurendon.

I'd never been in the new building. I'd driven past it occasionally when visiting my parents, but never gone inside. I had fragments of memories of the old village hall; numerous Christmas concerts, and friends' birthday parties. The new building looked very different, built from sandy brick with a flat zinc roof and plenty of glass, it was light and airy. We didn't go into the main hall but went straight to the admin offices. Whilst the records section of the old building had been totally destroyed in the fire, as it was so small, it couldn't hold all the archive material, dating back to when the records began. The older stuff had been stored in a lower level – like the undercroft of a church I suppose – a basement in modern terms, with stone walls and a vaulted ceiling. The fire hadn't got down into it, so if the Shadow Man had started the fire to destroy the oldest records, he'd failed miserably.

Now restored to a quiet side room, the records library contained every historic scrap of information recorded about the village and the surrounding area. Katie and I had phoned ahead and asked if we might spend some time there, and they were almost over-enthusiastic in their support. Perhaps nobody ever came in to the records room, with its cream-painted concrete block walls, industrial pipework and narrow walkways between floor-to-ceiling shelves – like the most unwelcoming library you'd ever seen. Perhaps they needed to demonstrate that each part of the building was being used and so worth its place. Whatever, we found ourselves plied with tea and coffee as we took over two large tables in the middle of the general library and spent some time ferrying large leather-bound volumes containing the history of the village from the records room to our camp. The volumes contained newspaper clippings, and then further back, notes, ledgers and records from the court or magistrate, since the first origins of the village. We'd pushed the two tables together and on one, ledgers, documents, dossiers and intriguing leather envelopes held closed by string were piled high. The other table became our workspace, each of us piling ledgers between our two open laptops. It was in one of these volumes that we found what we were looking for.

Katie cautiously turned a cardboard page, its contents covered in cellophane. 'It's all very fragile,' she said, 'be careful.' The ledgers still demanded care when you considered the age of the paper within. From what we could make out from the files and computer records, the village had been around since the twelfth century, when local barons – wealthy lords who owned land – brought in workers to farm the land and built a village on the hill. We found a record from 1725 noting more farms were built on the land. Two were built opposite each other on the junction of what is now Stow Lane and Lake Road, just along from the pond, which was obviously still in existence. Although back then, the lakes, created from quarrying in the 1960s and 70s, didn't exist and were just farmland. Other people set up home; labourers, a blacksmith, shopkeepers, a tavern and ultimately a school, and self-appointed community leaders began to record the events and legal happenings within the village. Several cuttings dating back to the later 1700s noted that a number of children had gone missing. They also noted that a number of people had burned to death as well, but didn't link the two. The records described searches of the land, of outbuildings and then dwelling places themselves. Everyone's home was searched, apart from the gentry. They failed to record the irony that if the killer was from more noble lineage, he would've got away scot-free. They did record that the search had progressed over time, until they had searched the home of William Tullock, a man described as 'strange' and who always 'kept himself to himself'. The next entry mentioned that clothing belonging to the missing children had been found in his house. An entry from the local magistrate noted that Tullock was detained and kept in chains in the cellar of the magistrate's house. A meeting there concluded that he must have taken the five children and kept some of their clothing as 'mementos.'

'He was a sick bastard,' Katie said, curling her lip in distaste.

'If it was him.'

'What do you mean?'

'Well, they've searched the home of a misfit guy, wouldn't have been warrants or requirements for evidence then.'

'And the clothing?'

'All inadmissible by today's standards, no forensics, no actual police force, just a hate mob and a kangaroo court.'

'So, he wasn't the killer then?'

'No, he might've been, but we'll never know, just that a committee decided he was.'

'Hang on, there's another entry here.' Katie moved to another page. 'It looks like they concluded that Tullock was also the 'prowler', seen periodically around the homes in the community at night. When children began to go missing, their peers began to call him the Shadow Man. They created a nursery rhyme in the belief that its recital would protect them from him.'

'Nursery rhyme? Like ours?' I said, frowning.

'Yeah.'

'No. We created that nursery rhyme. We did.'

'But it's written here – it's more old-fashioned, but it's the same thing. We can't have done.'

'That's fucked up – I know we wrote it, I remember being shit-scared one night and starting to say some lines and we all just joined in. How can we have known this rhyme in the first place to then start reciting it? Unless we'd heard it before – but I can't remember.'

'I don't see how any of us can have known this rhyme. But it's there in black and white.'

'So frustrating that there's still some blanks in my memory.'

'They burnt him at the stake, look.' Katie indicated an article on the next page, stating that 'the murderer, William Tullock, was taken to the island in the middle of the village pond and tied to a stake, around which was placed firewood and other timbers, and, after reading the charges thus proven against him, the fire was lit.'

'It says the whole village turned out to watch, and they cheered at his screams,' I said, continuing to read from the report.

'He was their first bogeyman.'

'And they got him.'

'Or they got someone.'

'Hey, take a look at this.' I pointed elsewhere on the page.

'What you got?'

'There's one entry that says his son, Daniel Tullock, was taken in by another family and his name changed to Teal.'

'Teal?'

'Yes, the family that adopted him changed his surname to theirs, but looking at these stories in the file, I don't think it worked out too well.'

'Show me.' Katie crowded in by my side to get a better look at the notes I was reading.

'Look here – there's an entry saying about a theft of some money and food, accusing Daniel Teal.'

'Then there's another about an attack on someone.'

'Then his new family disowns him, and he disappears.' I continued to flick through the volumes while Katie searched on the online library resources. Larger towns had extensive archives of their records, first on microfiche and latterly computer files for ease of storage. If we spent long enough, we essentially had access to the whole country.

'But maybe not,' Katie said pointing to a screengrab of a press clipping, 'Look here. The name of Teal, comes up over in the Vale – and then years later, even as far as Sheffield.'

'Yes, look, a story of a fire in some village and Daniel Teal was a suspect, but then the story dies and we see nothing more in this thread of cuttings. Anything on an internet search?'

'You'll need to give me a few minutes, Flip.'

'Okay. I'm gonna take some of this stuff back to the records room, give us a bit more space.' I piled up some of the leather volumes that we'd classed as 'done' and carried them carefully back to records, filing them where we'd found them. I returned and Katie had more to tell me.

'There's not enough logged from the news of that time for such a small place. As we said, there is some of Sheffield's big news – a huge fire in a mill for example. But no link to Teal.'

'You don't think the mill fire could be him?'

'Who knows, Flip. If you look at these search results here, there are stories down the years, though; interviews with a Teal at the scene of a fire, a Teal as a suspect where people have been burned to death. When you look at them and cross-reference the name, it's synonymous with arson and people dying.'

'Oh my fucking God, Jesus Christ. I've just thought of something.' A thought, a memory had just coalesced out of the fog. And it was terrifying.

'This is a hell of a time to get religion, sister.'

'Just let me get on the computer, will you?' We changed seats and I immediately started to type, searching on family names in the village – searching for confirmation of what I already knew. 'Fuck me.' I stared at the screen, my stomach turned and wretched, almost throwing its contents at the laptop.

'Oh my God, you're right.' Katie stared at the screen, the truth undeniable. I'd kind of half remembered it as soon as Katie mentioned Tullock's adopted name, and the memory had been gnawing away at me in the background, like the sound of a fly in your bedroom, buzzing all night until you really have to get up to deal with the bastard.

'Yep, Janey's mum's maiden name was Teal. Do you think she's related to him? Rather than to his adopted family, I mean?'

'Well of course she's related to him. He was the murdering arsonist wasn't he?'

'So Janey's descended from William Tullock. She's the Shadow Man.'

Chapter 20

– X –

The Circle of Fire

Triumph.

That was the look on Janey's face as I passed out. She was standing over us as if she'd won, and then the world disappeared from around me.

I had a dream. I dreamt I was laying on the ground, immobile, my hands tied and body sunk into a coffin-shaped hole.

You will forget, you will forget, you will forget.

Then I was aware of a smell, a stench, something strong and foul, like death and shit had teamed up to create a fragrance.

You will forget, you will forget, you will forget.

Then something was crawling over me, stinking of it, slimy and horrible, its cold body brushing against mine and I tried to flinch away, its touch so reprehensible and abhorrent. It whispered to me, chanted, like they were incantations or instructions.

You will forget, you will forget, you will forget.

I thought I'd gag, I thought that maybe I'd already choked on my own vomit, such was the smell and taste in my mouth.

Slowly my awareness returned, and the first thing I remember was a sound. I could hear a crackling and popping, the sound of a fire and I could feel its heat. The resin in the wood would suddenly explode with a spitting-bang as the fire roared away. I opened my eyes, head feeling like it was full of concrete. I was still laying on my side, my head tilted downwards at a sharp angle, stretching my neck painfully. The rough stone and gravel on the floor dug into the thin skin of my forehead, adding to the discomfort. I tried to move but my wrists were tied in front of me with baler twine. I could see two of the others, Katie and Clara, on either side of the fire, they too were lying on their sides on the ground, but they looked like they were still out. Behind me I heard someone coughing and retching, and I knew it was Sally, but I couldn't turn to look what state she was in. Still breathing would have to do for the moment. I tried to sit up, but my head was throbbing so hard, the pounding so painful, that the fog closed over me again, the sound of laughter fading away just as I passed out.

'Let me call Clara and Sal, we've gotta warn them.' I pulled out my phone. There were missed calls from both of them. A lot from Sal. 'Shit, something's happening. I hope we're not too late.' I called her number. It rang out four times before going to voicemail – I'd heard her outgoing message a few times in the last couple of weeks when organising this trip. But it had been changed, and all I heard on the message now was a scream. It was like Sal was in the same room, screaming in my ear. My blood turned to ice and my heart started to pound, the breath catching in my throat. 'She's got Sal,' I said.

As I was calling Sal, Katie called Clara to save time. She answered straightaway and Katie put her on speaker.

'Where are you?'

'I went for a walk. Janey asked Sal to help her sort some clothes out. Felt like three was a crowd so I've walked round the village. Heading back to the pub now as it goes. What've you found?'

'Janey's the Shadow Man,' Katie said.

'Fuck off, is she?' Clara almost laughed at us down the phone line.

'Her mother's maiden name is Teal, and the son of the guy who was burned at the stake for *being* the Shadow Man changed his name to Teal.'

'Shit. No way.'

'There've been Teals around burnings across the north of England for two hundred years,' I said.

'It's like a family business,' Katie added.

'Oh my God, Sal.' I could hear the terror in Clara's voice.

'Get to the pub and I'll pick you up – we're almost at the car now.'

I screeched to a halt beside Clara and she jumped into the Land Rover. I roared off, sending chippings and tufts of grass from the verge flying as I did so.

'Where're we going?' Clara asked.

'Janey's. Gotta see if they're still there.'

'And if they are?'

'Let's worry about that when we get there,' I said tearing along Stow Road, drawing some disapproving looks from local pedestrians. I pulled up outside Janey's house, parked halfway up the pavement and we all got out at a run, sprinting to her porch door as fast as we could.

'Janey. Are you there? Let us in, babe,' Katie got there first, banging hard on the door with her palm. I checked the windows round the back but couldn't see anyone home. The strange dark polytunnel jutted out like a witch's nose from the back of the place. While Katie continued to bang on the door, Clara looked underneath cracked and neglected plant pots – but why would anyone who never went out hide a spare key? An old concrete block sat at the base of the garden wall. Abandoned and unused for decades it was now a home to a healthy culture of moss and a shelter for woodlice and earwigs. I bent and picked up the heavy object, grunting as I did and heaving it against my chest. Woodlice fell away and a millipede ran up my arm as I wheezed another breath. Gripping the concrete firmly I twisted my body away from the door then turned quickly to smash the heavy weight against the side of the lock and door handle. There was a breaking sound and the door flew open, a piece of PVC the length of the door splintered from the side of the lock and cartwheeled off into the kitchen.

'Nice,' said Katie poking her head round the door. 'Let's get in here and see if anyone's at home. We split up and quickly checked each room – the house was empty – Janey and Sal had gone.

'Okay let's see if we can find anything.' I nodded at the others. Clara made a start in the kitchen and 'middle' room while Katie went to the lounge, leaving me with Janey's bedroom. It looked exactly the same as when I'd snooped around when we first got here a thousand years ago, but now I realised what I was seeing. I'd seen the black trilby on the corner of the noticeboard but hadn't given it any more thought until now. It was the hat that Janey had worn as the Shadow Man. The one – or one like it – that she'd worn when she'd attacked Luke that day, and worn in the rain in my front garden. It had been hung up in her room for all to see since we arrived. She must've used the black scarf hung alongside it to cover her face – only Luke had seen her up close and might've realised that someone was underneath.

Those days. I'd been terrified of a wraith or a spirit when really it was someone I'd called friend.

I stood at the small table looking down at the crude model of the lake. It was like she'd been re-enacting the events of years before. I looked up at the notice-board, reading the stories and newspaper clippings. Story after story of burnings and fatal fires across the country. These clippings were all about her. Not an interest or an obsession but a legacy – a diary of murder and terror. I reached up to the cork board and pulled down a faded, grainy picture. It was hard to tell because of its age, but it looked like a newspaper snap that some local hack had taken at Janey's parent's funeral – God knows why they thought that was newsworthy.

'That's odd,' I found myself saying out loud.

'What is?' called Clara.

'Come and look at this picture.' Clara hurried into the bedroom and I handed her the image.

'It's Janey dressed in black. What are you getting at?' Clara looked at me, shaking her head.

'Well, this is Janey at the graveside, right?'

'It looks like that. And look at her, she's got this calm look on her face. She almost looks happy,' Clara held the picture between thumb and forefinger as if she might get contaminated by it.

'Yeah but look again. She said she was fat, that she'd been in a mess, mentally, leading up to her parent's death and got really fat. So she would've been overweight at their funeral. But here she is looking as slim as ever.' Clara and I exchanged a glance.

'What are you thinking?' she asked.

'Okay, I'll search her parents' room – bedside cabinets, dressing tables and all that. You do the bathroom cabinet.'

'What am I looking for?'

'Tablets.'

We split up and I headed straight for the dressing table in Mr and Mrs Pullman's room. I went through the drawers, finding his and hers underwear, socks and tights, vests, scarves and t-shirts. Janey hadn't thrown anything away. I took the briefest of glimpses in the wardrobe and found nothing of note, although there were quite a few shoeboxes that we might need to check. On to the bedside cabinets. On one side was Arthur C Clarke, a comb, a packet of condoms – which sent all kinds of weird thoughts going through my head – and some Rennies. On the other side of the bed was Jackie Collins – much racier than my mum's Mills and Boon – some hand cream and a hair net.

'What've you got?' asked Clara walking into the bedroom.

'A weird sense of going back in time to see things that no one has used for twenty-five to thirty years, yet here we all are.'

'What?'

'Things. Stuff. The things you use every day that you need like a comb or a hair net or a book. All left here, like you were going to come back into the room that evening. It's like a museum to them. It makes me want to cry remembering all my parents' stuff that was like this. I got rid of it all and I could've kept it. But it also freaks me out that she's left it frozen in time like this.'

'Did you find any pills?'

'What? No,' I said bringing myself back to reality.

'Neither did I, beyond paracetamol and ibuprofen. What are you so keen on finding pills for, anyway?'

'Janey said her folks were terminally ill and so they went off for their little day trip without her. But if you're that ill, you must be on a shitload of meds. Fuck, even just a few pills – decent painkillers or stuff to stop you feeling sick or something. But there's nothing above paracetamol here.'

'Maybe she cleared them out?'

'She clear out anything else?' I thought about the Rennies and the condoms. 'No. But that means she was lying about her parents. She's just killed them, and –'

'– she must be lying about everything else.'

A bang and a clank jolted us back to reality from Keyser Söze-land and I poked my head out of the bedroom. Katie was standing by the back door with the concrete block in her hands after using it to smash the padlock off the door to Janey's mushroom farm.

'Flip, you better come and take a look at this,' Katie's voice shook – completely out of character for her.

'What is it?' I said, approaching along the hallway and looking through the now smashed doorway into the gloom created by the polytunnel room. 'Oh Christ.' At first glance it was laid out like a greenhouse – rows of shelves on the three available sides, all containing long plastic boxes full of soil. Janey's mushroom propagation was well-organised, with each shelf containing mushrooms at a different stage of growth – the lower shelves had specimens just erupting from the soil, the middle shelves were more fully developed and the top shelves were bare soil. A complex sprinkler system was set up with small grey pipes bolted just above the boxes with spray bars to keep the soil moist. The pipes all congregated on the wall in a large manifold with a digital timer. Overhead lighting hung down above each of the rows of boxes, illuminating them at a low and precise level. This was the cutting edge of fungiculture and something that Janey had obviously gone to a lot of time and effort to research and set up.

'How could she do all this if she doesn't go out? Can you get all this online?' asked Clara.

'She doesn't not go out though, does she?' I said. 'That's all bullshit. It's a lie to make us think of her one way and never suspect what she really is.'

'Christ yes, how stupid am I?'

'It's been a long day already.'

'What if more of it's bullshit?' asked Katie.

'Like what?' I asked turning to face her. 'She isn't faking her injuries, you can't fake those scars.'

'Well, you could, but I don't think she is. We know she lost her leg, too. But what about faking the pain that she's in? Maybe that's a lie to add to the legend too?'

'So why all this?' I pointed toward the shelves.

'But in that case, why *that*?' Katie pointed at the floor. Elevated on some four-by-two timber lengths was a large wooden box half-full of soil which was quite well compacted in places. There was a small table next to it with a lamp that Janey hadn't switched off and which was throwing a gloomy light across this end of the room. Nearest us was a pillow in a pink pillowcase that was faded from repeated trips through the washing machine, and a duvet thrown back across the lower part of the box had a matching cover. Janey slept in a box full of soil, all cosy under a blanket and comfortable on her pillow, surrounded by the damp wetness of the soil nurturing her magic mushrooms. *This* was Janey's bedroom.

My phone beeped as I received a message. *The top lake. Time's running out and the Shadow Man's here.* We were two steps behind her, unable to anticipate her next move, falling into a series of traps she'd laid for us. Right back to when she contacted us asking about the dreams. She must've done something to us to make us forget and then remember.

I thought back to my dream, and the voice telling me I must forget, I must forget. I remembered then that I was stoned on mushrooms at the time. She'd used it as a form of hypnosis. I'd read somewhere that people who'd dropped acid twenty years ago could still get flashbacks to bad trips they'd had even now. And maybe that's what was happening here. Maybe she'd set something up, to trigger us, ready for this moment.

Janey wants us up at the top lake?

Let's not keep her waiting.

I don't know how long I was out for, probably only a matter of seconds, but the noise of the fire seeped into my consciousness to rouse me once again. The cold gravel floor dug into head and left shoulder where I'd fallen over, and the pain served to bring me around properly. I tried to sit up, but my arms would barely work, I was groggy and my mouth tinder dry. I managed to lever myself upright, my eyes fixated on the flames, my back complaining, and my legs stiff from being twisted underneath me.

'Welcome back, Flip.' It was Janey's voice somewhere above me, slowly drifting into my head.

My head.

Which weighed as much as a car slowly cranked itself upright and there she was, beside the fire. She stood alert and totally naked, her body covered in the stinking mud from the lake, smeared all over her, pulled through her hair so it stood in spikes and covering all but her eyes. 'Always a bit behind, but nothing new there, is there?' Her voice was different, stronger, bitter and more aggressive than she'd ever sounded.

'What's going on?' I managed to mumble, my lips sticking together.

'Well, let's see. Luke here is very glad that I've let him out of the workshop – apparently being left alone there for a few days can really do your head in.'

'Fucking bitch.' It was the first notice I'd taken of the naked figure kneeling at Janey's feet. Luke Lewis was bound with ropes running round his chest in several loops, disappearing behind him running lengthways down his body going under his crotch. He was kneeling in quite a flexed position with his hands behind his back and it looked like they must be tied back there.

'Thank you darling, now shut up or I'll cut your balls off.' She almost spat the words into his face as she cradled his chin in her hands. 'Now, where was I? Oh yes. Luke is about to become another victim of the Shadow Man, and I'm not quite sure what to do with you lot yet.'

You will forget, you will forget, you will forget.

'But we're your friends, Janey.' I sounded whiney, like I was pleading, and I guess I was, but I was trying to sound strong, to appeal to her better nature, the side of her I knew. But maybe, you never really know anyone at all.

'If I have to tolerate another minute in your company, Flip, I swear I'll cut my own fucking arm off. The only reason I ever wanted to be around you was to give me a cover story, so nobody would suspect me.'

'What?'

'You and your future middle-class friends, all planning to leave this place sooner or later – when you get a job or marry a nice man or go to fucking university. Not caring about the past, about history, justice, and the people you'll leave behind – people who can't leave.'

'I'm sorry Janey, I've got no idea what you're talking about,' I said, as gently as I could, not wanting to rile her.

'Of course you fucking don't. You can barely see the nose on your face. No, hey, how about we cut that pretty nose of yours off later, hmmm?'

I was really scared now.

'You're the Shadow Man?' I was incredulous.

'None other.'

'But why?'

'Two hundred years ago the people of this village framed my ancestor for crimes he never committed. They tortured him and burned him alive. They hounded him and framed him for anything bad that went on here – and a lot of bad things were going on. All of my life he's spoken to me, been with me, been my strength, my inner voice. And now I'm giving him something back.'

'So there was no Shadow Man?'

'Oh yeah there was, and the kids did make up a nursery rhyme – the book I told you about was real. It didn't only apply here in Laurendon, Will was a legend throughout the whole area. When I told you, I wanted it to be specific to *here*.'

'Just to do *this*? To entice us in?'

'To bring this village down. We'll destroy this place, Will and me, brick by fucking brick.'

∞ ∞ ∞

I didn't care that Janey's door wouldn't shut properly. Any opportunistic burglar would be in for a bit of a surprise and at some point the police would come by and piece things together. We should probably call them, make it official.

But what exactly would we say? Would we be able to convince a weary copper that we'd all got together over the weekend and discovered our long-lost disabled friend was pretending to be a two-hundred-year-old wraith coming back for revenge on the village and the villagers that had persecuted him?

We climbed into my car and drove off with a screech of tyres. Driving by the familiar houses it struck me that this village had been the canvas on which I'd painted my childhood. That my memories of us riding around and going to the lake and of belonging and a lack of responsibilities had been a veneer. A veneer to cover despair and failure and death.

I looked at the buildings as we drove by – older houses that I knew, although, for the most part, I couldn't remember who'd lived in them back then, and certainly wouldn't know who lived in them now. Newer houses interspersed in ones and twos or as little three bungalow cul-de-sacs. It made me sad to think of how the village had changed. Not *the* village, my village. *My hometown* as Springsteen would say.

But it belonged to other people now. It was very different to the Laurendon I'd called home, more houses, fewer farms and the industry around them, more commuters wanting to live away from Sheffield, Doncaster and Leeds amidst leafy farmland. This was theirs and I didn't belong here anymore.

Unless it belonged to someone else, someone who wasn't going to up and leave after a few years, someone who had always been here, who had never left and never would, not even in death. He had always watched over the place, for good or for bad. Who had the greatest claims to this place? Me? The current residents? Or Will Tullock, the Shadow Man?

I drove up to the gate on the farm road.

'Can you get the gate open, Clara?'

'Okay, I'll take a look,' she jumped out of the car before it stopped and ran toward the closed gate – the chain was looped through the gate catch. 'There's no getting through this without the key, Flip,' she shouted back.

'We'll see. Stand back.' I revved the engine and reversed the car back thirty yards.

'What are you doing?' Katie said from the back seat.

'Taking route one.' I replied

'You've got to be fucking kidding me! Why can't we walk?'

'There isn't time, not now that psycho has Sal.' Taking one look at the middle of the large farm gate I gunned the engine again, slid her into first gear and roared forward with my foot flat to the floor. I hit the gate at thirty. Two tons of Britain's finest engineering hit the centre of the gate, there was a huge jarring crash, the car paused for the briefest of seconds until the shockwave of momentum and inertia bent and splintered the oak, buckling it outwards as the front third of the Discovery crumpled inwards and the airbag prevented me rearranging my face on the steering wheel. Then we were through, the gate breaking in half and bursting open, and I drove on another twenty yards before skidding to a halt on the rutted track, throwing a cloud of dust up around us like a skirt.

Clara ran up to the passenger side and jumped in. 'Go,' she said as she reached to grab the door, looking across at me pushing the deflating remains of the airbag out of the way, slamming the door shut as the tyres span on the dirt track. The sun was sinking, a blazing ball on the horizon as I raced along the lane, bouncing in and out of the ruts, Clara and Katie thrown around in their seats. I grimly hung on to the steering wheel as it was wrenched around, threatening to pull away from my grasp and dash us against huge tree trunks or old farm buildings. The sunset illuminated the surface of our lake as we roared past, the noise sending a flock of Canada geese into a panic, taking off into the red sun like a squadron of Hueys in *Platoon*. Up the slope we drove, the track becoming a little easier with fewer ruts and I drew to a halt at the top by the fence. Looking across we could see a huge raging fire on the gravel beside the cave entrance. We forced ourselves through the fence once again and approached the two figures illuminated by the flames.

'Sorry girls,' muttered Sal, through swollen, blood-encrusted lips.

Janey, standing beside her, said nothing.

'How the hell did you get out here?' Katie asked.

'She's got a car, hasn't she!' said Sal, spitting blood on the floor. *What the hell had Janey done to her?*

'What?' I said.

'What the fuck?' added Clara, noticing the Ford Focus parked at the other end of the plateau, its boot open.

'Oh, you think because I lied about some stuff I'd tell the truth about everything else? You really are stupid,' sneered Janey, her good eye blinking contempt.

'But I thought you never went out?' I asked.

'I usually go out at night and nobody really *looks* at me, nobody knows me. They might've heard of an odd recluse with a fucked-up face who lives on Stow Road, but that's it. I'm totally anonymous. It's hiding in plain sight. This really isn't a sleepy little village any more – and I'm a stranger.

'I remember now, I remember who you are and what you did to Luke Lewis.'

'Congratulations,' came the half smile.

'What do you mean, Flip?' asked Katie. I looked at her, my returning memory forgetting that she wouldn't have known.

'Yeah, just what the fuck happened?' echoed Clara.

'Why don't you tell our friends what happened, Flip.' She said my name with a pause in the middle, making it sound like fur-lip.

'Janey's long-lost ancestor…'

'William Tullock. You're welcome.'

'Yeah him. He was the Shadow Man. He killed all those kids and burned people two hundred years ago.'

'But that's the point, you stupid bitch, he didn't kill them. They framed him – set him up because he was a weird loner – and they killed him.'

'And you know this, because...?' I asked.

'Because it's obvious, Flip. He was a scapegoat. They weren't interested in finding who did it, just on blaming someone. Besides, he told me.'

'He told you?'

'Not gonna get very far just repeating everything I say, Katie. Yes, he told me. He's been with me in my head for as long as I can remember, but I didn't really understand or know what to do until that summer, until Ethel Grimshaw.'

∞ ∞ ∞

'How does he speak to you?' I asked, my head slowly beginning to clear.

'In here,' smiled Janey pointing to her temple. 'Now if you'd kindly shut the fuck up, I've gotta kill Luke here.' She aimed a kick at the small of Luke's back. And, like a caged lion, he roared at her in frustration, straining at his bonds. He tried to stand, leaning forward, bent double and struggled against the rope tied to the metal frame of the workshop. He managed to get both feet under him in a squatting positon and slowly started to straighten up, muscles bulging against his restraints. Janey appeared in front of him. 'Take the weight off, there's a love,' and kneed him hard in the balls, her hands cradling his chest as he fell forward, his body bending and buckling, releasing the tension against the rope which jerked him back to the floor, landing on his knees and falling forward to face plant with a crunch onto the gravel. He roared again, frustrated and angry, lashing out with a leg, and trying to look up, but his face was now covered in blood and gravel and soil. Janey went to the side of the workshop and put on a pair of gardening gloves, before picking up the nozzle attached to the old red diesel tank. She pointed it at Luke and pulled the trigger, the gravity-fed pump splashing old fuel onto Luke's face, then in a steady stream poured all over his body. When he was thoroughly doused in the fuel she released the trigger, holding the nozzle like a gun, ready and waiting to be used again.

Waiting for us.

Janey brought the diesel pump down to Luke's tied wrists, enclosing his fingers in her gloved hands to wrap them around the handle, leaving his fingerprints. 'No!' he roared, straining once again against his bonds, he looked up and the diesel ran off his head into his eyes, and his cries must've been of stinging pain as well as fear of what was about to happen. He lunged at Janey, his wide shoulder striking her, his hand pulling the trigger of the pump behind him causing fuel to splash all down her.

'Fuck, you'll pay for that, you idiot,' Janey sneered at him, making vague efforts to brush excess fuel from her body. It soaked into the drying mud and even washed some away from her leg. Peeling his hands away from the pump and dispensing with the nozzle, she picked up a heavy plumbers' wrench and swung it at his head like a club, but Luke ducked at the last minute and she only managed to catch him a glancing blow. It was enough to leave him stunned but not incapacitated like she'd probably hoped. Janey stood over the panting, raging form of would-be rapist Luke Lewis, appearing in two minds about what to do. She noticed me out of the corner of her eye. Looking back and forth between us, she raised the wrench again and swung it backhanded to hit me on the side of the head with enough force to knock me over onto my side again. My senses were reeling from the blow, the dizziness rising again and I could feel myself starting to fall, the ground opening underneath me and I knew I had to stay awake, to stay with the scene and not let myself go, because then Janey would have me. I didn't know whether I was passing out or if I was dying, but I fought as best I could, concentrating on the tableau before me. As I lay there struggling against unconsciousness, the last thing I saw was Luke lunge at Janey, who was standing right by his side. His skin all wet and shiny from the diesel, he'd managed to get one leg underneath him again as Janey struck me, and now he seemed to propel himself up and forwards like a jack-in-the-box, striking her in the midriff with his head and propelling them both into the fire, which, fed by the liquid fuel, rose to engulf them like an inferno.

Chapter 21

— X —

When is it Not Too Late?

'And now his weird, loner descendant is gonna get revenge for him. Is that it?' Katie couldn't stop the contempt in her voice.

'Just what the fuck has this got to do with us?' spat Clara.

Janey reached down into her cloth holdall and pulled out a shotgun, pointing it in our direction. 'Anything else fucking clever to say?' She almost screamed the words, the shotgun barrel shaking in her hands. 'You were never my friends, you just felt sorry for me.'

'That's not true. We stayed friends from the village school to comp. We didn't find other groups of people there because we didn't quite fit in, did we? Bunch of misfits, Janes, all of us, which was why it was cool that we had each other.'

'Oh, but didn't you, Katie, refer to me as *the freak*?' The barrel of the gun swung in Katie's direction.

'And didn't I get called *the tits*, and sometimes *the slapper*?' Katie replied bitterly. 'They were just words, Janey, just names, nicknames, badges of honour, maybe. That's all.'

'Not by me. *Never* by me.' Janey's eyes were intense with anger and something else. Madness maybe. 'I never called you any bad names.'

'If it upset you, Janey, we're sorry,' Clara apologised quietly.

'Everything has consequences, doesn't it?' sneered Janey.

'Where'd you get the gun, Janey?' I asked.

'It was Dad's,' she smiled, waving the barrel round in a figure of eight motion. 'He used to go with Stuart MacFarlane on his shoot. Kept the gun locked in the loft – knew it would come in handy.'

'So taking care of us is closure then is it?' I had no idea how to handle this, no idea whether she was focused, deranged or could be reasoned with or not. But I had to try.

'Something like that.' Janey hefted the barrel of the gun onto her shoulder, still maintaining a grip on the trigger.

'And then what?'

'What's that supposed to mean?'

'You've been stewing, in your parents' house, recovering from your injuries and starting to hear the voices.'

'Watch your mouth, Flip. I told you, I've always heard them. I only *understood* them after the accident.'

'Wasn't really an accident, though was it?'

'What?'

'An accident is not braking in time and hitting the car in front of you, or barging into someone in the pub. Kidnapping someone with the intention of burning them to death and it going tits-up isn't really an accident, is it?'

'I saved your arse when I took Luke Lewis. You even said thank you, you stupid cow. And of course I was the flavour of the month – in the paper and everything,' Janey did her half sneer. 'Brave girl that took on the bully and gets her leg burnt off. I was the hero of the hour in 'saving' all of you from Luke.' Janey paced up and down on the same gravel as she had all those years before, looking taller, bolder than she had at her house. Her limp was gone. 'And it shut his bleating parents up from going on about what a saint he was when he was missing.'

'And did they ever recover? Wasn't really their fault, was it?' I said.

'He wasn't their *fault*? Then who's was he?'

'And that's when I started having the dreams, after your accident. I didn't have them that summer – they came later. They were memories of what you did.'

'And I started having them too,' said Clara. 'But I reckon I was stoned out of my head at the top lake and I don't remember anything. Maybe I passed out. Maybe I did take something in, but when I heard the story the next day, and there was you, Janey, with your leg and your face, I remember that's when I started dreaming.'

'The farmer called the emergency services when he saw the fire,' said Sal, as if it was now becoming clear.

'This is good – role reversal, because I don't remember anything.' Janey smiled at them.

'First the fire brigade came then an ambulance and the police.'

'I didn't realise at the time, but pretty much straight away the police said it was Luke that had tried to kill Janey, and I was gonna be next,' I said.

'They'd heard the stories that he wanted to get back at you Flip, and decided he must've gone crazy or something,' said Katie.

'I don't think there was a lot left of him – all the ropes he was tied with burnt away.'

'But you were awake, Flip. Why didn't you remember?' asked Sal.

'I don't know. I kept phasing in and out. Janey must've said something to me.'

You will forget, you will forget, you will forget.

Janey laughed at them piecing the puzzle together. 'Dead easy, really, the power of suggestion when someone is stoned and pissed. I kept whispering to you all when you were laying there.'

'And that's why I dreamed of something crawling over me smelling of that awful mud from the lake.'

'You say the nicest things.'

'I came to see you once in the hospital. It was weird – horrible. You were covered in bandages but you were saying really strange things – now I know, it was like you were Will and he was speaking though you. It was the same when they put you in the ambulance at the lake, but I just thought you were manic because of the pain you were in. It scared the life out of me, like something from the Exorcist, and I never visited again.'

'You all dropped me pretty quickly, didn't you, and yet you say you were my friends.'

'It wasn't like that. School re-started. It was busy. I never seemed to have time,' said Katie.

'Didn't have time for me, that's for certain.'

'It just drifted, Janey, and you can't say it wasn't unusual circumstances,' said Katie.

'But you killed those people that summer when you didn't understand the voice, right?' I said.

'Yes. It was more by accident, really.'

'You 'accidentally' killed Mrs Grimshaw?'

'I just broke into her place – it wasn't that hard, the lock was shit and I forced it easily. And that was it. I was standing in her room, and there she was, laying on her back, snoring like a bastard. She'd threatened to kill my dog. *My* dog. She had sleep apnoea and slept with an oxygen supply, so I turned it off and waited until she passed out. I'd thought about putting a pillow over her head, but I'd read so much about myths and legends and come across the Shadow Man story that I just had to burn her.'

'So you didn't know about your ancestor then?'

'No, I'd just found the book about him, I didn't make a link between that and the voice until later.'

'How did you make it look like an accident?'

'She'd got cigarettes by the side of the bed, I lit one and used it to set light to the bottom of her nightie. It didn't burn like I thought, it kind of reacted, like when you watch those magnesium experiments in school, or put a piece of sodium on water. The flame kind of fizzed across her nightdress like a ripple, and melted to her – you could see it tightening and wrapping round her like a tentacle or something. And it was meltingly hot – I guess it cooked the bitch like wrapping her in tin foil. Must've took hours.'

'So why didn't the rest of the room go up?'

'I'm not sure, but because her nightie melted to her it was slow – there wasn't really any flame. The heat must've been so intense underneath her that it melted her dress to the nylon sheet and it became a hard plastic shell. It must've protected the rest of the mattress, so only her body burned. It was pure luck the whole thing looked like some sort of supernatural human combustion thing.'

'And Todd Ainsworth?'

'He was easy. He was parked up in his car just off Stow Road. I used to go cycling a lot at night and I saw him. He was smoking dope in his car, the window open. So I chloroformed him.'

'Chloroform?' asked Clara. 'F. O.'

'I'd stolen a jar from school so I could use it on frogs before I dissected them – seeing their beating hearts was cool.'

'Jesus.'

'I used paraffin on Todd, less reactive than petrol, so I just soaked his shirt and lit him with his own joint. He had leather seats in his car and they didn't burn, so once the shirt and his body went up, the fire kind of died.'

'Another unexplained fire,' said Clara.

'It was amazing. There's no way you could fake that, it was just pure luck.'

'I'm sure Mrs Grimshaw and Todd would've appreciated that.'

'Oh come on – not wanting to speak ill of the dead are we? Old lady Grimshaw was an evil bastard and we all thought it. None of us were sorry when she croaked. And Todd was a creep – the world was a better place without him.'

'Oh you're a real public servant, you are,' Katie fired back.

'Easy, Katie,' I said.

'Why? Because if we piss her off she might want to *really* kill us, instead of just killing us?'

'Ladies. I'm supposed to be the insane serial killer in the group.'

'Every group's got one,' muttered Katie.

'Why bring us back? Why us?'

'I brought you back, Flip, because *you* got to leave. I didn't. This place *does* eat you up, it has got something bad at its core.'

'It's just a village, Janey, with a village mentality and all, but that's it.'

'It's like a cancer hanging over the whole place, a darkness, and it's intertwined with Will, with me as his only family. I have to destroy this place.'

'But you could've left. You could've done your exams, got you're a levels and gone to university. Or just left – you don't need fucking A levels to move away, Janey, or a degree for god's sake.'

'It was too late for me then. I was just starting to walk again when you fucked off.'

'You'd got away with murder, like four times over, and with burning the village hall down. If that didn't kick start you trying to do something with your life, I don't know what would.'

'I couldn't leave. By the time you'd gone I'd found out who I was, and Will was in my head. I couldn't leave him alone in the village.'

'And your parents?'

'They were just getting in the way – increasingly so. It wasn't difficult to trick them to go for a drive as a way of getting me out of the house – they were delighted. And I chloroformed them too.'

'Jesus,' said Clara.

'And so Will Tullock is still in there pulling your strings?'

'He was. Not so much, now.'

'He's gone?'

'Yep. All those years ago he used to talk to me, the Shadow Man. But he hasn't for a long time.'

'For how long?'

'Not very much since that night.'

'When you killed Luke?'

'Yes. He has spoken to me since, but just snippets, like flying visits into my head. It seems like he didn't need to be around anymore.'

'But you were, weren't you?' I watched the prone form of Sal at Janey's feet and I was angry, almost forgetting the predicament we were in, but after two episodes of this over half a lifetime, it was time to stop her game.

Janey smiled at me, quizzically, pausing and trying to read my expression, wondering where I was going with this. 'Go on.'

'You didn't stop – we've seen dozens of reports from over the years – they aren't that hard to find when you really look across local papers on the web. People burning to death at home or in their cars.'

'Fires do happen.'

'But they smell of you, every one of them smells as bad as this lake. They were you weren't they?'

'Hey, I didn't set every fire that killed people in the north of England in the last thirty years…' A smile slowly spread across half of her face. 'But I did do a lot of them, you're right.'

'But why, though?'

'People excluded me from the word go.'

'Who excluded you – we certainly didn't. What the hell are you talking about?' Katie said with some anger in her voice.

'Let's just keep calm about this, we don't want… anyone to do anything rash.' I said.

'Fuck calm, I've just about had enough of this. She's gonna kill us because she felt left out and didn't have any friends, even though we were her friends. It makes no sense.'

'You weren't my friends, though, idiot. You might've thought you were, but I didn't. I never once called for you or phoned to see what you were doing. Hanging around with you did keep Will quiet though, which was good because he could be awfully noisy in my head, like all the bloody time. I needed a distraction.' Janey had lowered the muzzle of the shotgun. 'I'd always known I was different – the voice inside me told me so. When I heard about Will I could identify with his excommunication, with his isolation, and so we were kindred spirits I suppose. That's how he found me. When he left, and people were even more unpleasant because of the way I looked, I didn't see any reason to stop. People are stupid, people are nasty, and so I burn them.'

'But there is no 'he', Janey. It's all you, don't you see? You're not well and you need help. You need some treatment before it's too late.'

'At which point,' Janey said indicating Sal at her feet, and spinning around with her arms raised to indicate all she had created for tonight, 'does this constitute 'not too late'? It's very sweet of you, but if I keep doing this, it's the only way to keep a link to Will, it's the only way he'll see me. He's the only relative who really cared about me.'

'You couldn't have had more loving parents.'

'That's fucking bullshit! I couldn't have had more controlling parents. I couldn't have had parents who wanted me to be more like a Stepford daughter than they did. Do this, make friends here, go to these people's houses. Instead of sitting down and getting to know me, and spending time with me, about what made me tick, they tried to mould me into something else.'

'So instead of an imaginary friend, you made up an imaginary relative.'

'He wasn't fucking imaginary!' She spat at me, her mouth frothing with anger, as the shotgun waved around wildly and could've taken any one of us out in an instant.

'Just be careful with that thing.'

'And you be careful with that.' She pointed at me. 'Could always get you in trouble, that mouth of yours, Flip.'

'I still don't see why, though. I don't see why you have to get to us.'

'No, you don't, do you. You really aren't as smart as everyone thinks you are. Will Tullock was the first generation of my family in this village and I'm the last. He's trapped here and so am I. It's come completely full circle.'

'And so taking out everybody you ever knew closes things off, does it?' asked Katie, unable to keep the disdain from her voice.

'Something like that, yes.'

'But what now. What about after we've gone, Janey?' I asked.

'Will hasn't said.'

'He hasn't said very much over the fucking years by the sound of it, Toots,' Katie snapped.

'Yeah but he will. He'll see what I'm doing and he'll come back – I know he will. Then we'll decide what to do.'

'Are you saying that you're going to keep doing this until that voice tells you to stop?' Katie asked.

'Yes.'

'Well, and don't take this the wrong way, but what if that voice is all in your head?'

'It *is* all in my head, but it's not my voice. Think that I don't think I'm crazy? Fucking right I am, but taking revenge is the right thing to do. Now, if you'll excuse me, I don't want my fire to die down.'

∞ ∞ ∞

Janey bent forward awkwardly, her knee not easily flexing, and she picked up the paraffin can, with a spout already fitted. She quickly realised that she couldn't pour the fuel over Sal whilst keeping hold of the shotgun, so she carefully laid the weapon on her kit bag. Her hands free, Janey started shaking the paraffin over her old friend. Sal lay quietly on the ground, her only reaction to cough and spit when the pungent liquid splashed on her face.

'Janey, you don't have to do this, we can sort something out,' said Katie, taking a step closer.

'Don't come any closer, Tits, otherwise I'll throw this can in the fire and she'll go up like a match.'

'But you're gonna do it anyway,' Katie stole a quick glance at me, throwing her eyes to the left, twice, to make sure I knew what she meant. 'So why shouldn't we be a 'have-a-go' hero.' Katie spread her arms wide to the side, and I stole a couple of steps away from her as Janey was transfixed.

'Wanna go out in a blaze of glory, do you?' Janey was clearly enjoying this, enjoying the power she had over us, liberated now that we knew who she was.

'I always did like Bon Jovi,' said Katie. I took another couple of steps around Janey, then stood motionless again. It did put the fire between

Janey and me, so I'd have to go further round again to have a straight run at her, not that I had a plan for after that.

'You always did think you were a funny cow. Alright. See how you like this.' Janey picked up the shotgun again and awkwardly side footed the paraffin can so it skidded across the gravel to Katie's feet. 'Douse yourself in that,' she said.

'Fuck you.'

'Don't do it,' said Clara.

Janey fired the shotgun over Katie's head. 'Still want to sound clever, do you? Pour it over your fucking head, or the next shot is at your chest.' I ducked at the shotgun blast but used it as a chance to move just the other side of the fire. It was pitch dark now and Janey's entire focus was on Katie and making sure she had her where she wanted her. I had a clear run at Janey from the back and side and could also see Sal, lying on the ground at her feet.

Katie picked up the petrol can and inverted it over her head, the stinging acrid liquid flowing down over her, drenching her shirt and a dark wet stain appearing over her jeans as it ran.

'That's better.'

'You know you won't get away with this,' said Clara, defiantly.

'Oh? Who's gonna stop me?'

Two things happened at once. I decided that Janey's distraction was the perfect opportunity for me to run at her and I started off at a sprint. At the same moment, Sal decided to fight back and, even constrained as she was by the chains across her chest looping behind her back, she rolled backwards and kicked out at her captor. Janey took the blow in her crotch, causing her to gasp for breath and double over, bringing her eyes around in a low arc and she looked right at me rushing toward her. She swung the shotgun around, losing all interest in Katie and focusing on my charging run. In slow motion the barrel looped over Sal's supine form as she wriggled to get some balance so she could aim another kick. The barrel swept past the fire, the flames reflected off the polished metal, and slowly came around to aim at me. I was maybe eight yards away, and hurdled some of the debris that had fallen away from the fire, the searing heat burning the right side of my face, my legs protesting at being asked to perform to this level. Three yards away and there was an explosion in front of me, Janey firing the shotgun at point blank range, the muzzle blast blinding me for a second. Somehow, call it self-preservation, or my *spider sense*, I twisted as it fired, turning my shoulders away so they were more side on. Janey was going for the middle of my chest, but instead peppered my shoulder with shot, every single one causing white hot pain to go deep inside me. As the gun went off, small sparks ignited around us, like resin spitting from a fire, they exploded in the air like miniature fireworks and faded as soon as they appeared. I immediately felt my chest clog, as if someone had closed the hatches on Number 1 lung and I tried to heave a breath that wasn't coming. My vision started to fade with the pain and the immediate concern that my lung was collapsing, and I might've fallen but my momentum saw me crash into Janey, my elbow catching her in the throat, causing her to stagger back. I'd planned everything – peeling away from the rest of the group, quietly finding a straight line from where I could attack and then planned my run. I'd not given any thought at all to how to deal with her when we met. Janey pulled the shotgun up to waist level, aiming straight for my belly, a macabre grin in half her face and pulled the trigger. Nothing happened.

'Shit,' she said, letting the barrel drop. She'd fired twice and needed to re-load. More sparks crackled across the fuel-charged air, tiny pockets of fumes so concentrated that the extreme heat from the fire was enough to ignite them but not light up the whole area – Sal included. Janey tossed the gun into the air, catching it by the barrel and hefted it like a club, coming at me to cave my head in with the stock. Then came the kick. Sal had finally managed to get some leverage when she wasn't rolling back and forth on her hands and could now swing her leg with force and power. Janey saw it coming this time and turned to aim her own vicious kick at Sal's stomach. She crumpled on impact, groaning and curling up like an autumn leaf. I felt my foot brush against something heavy and looked down to see the monkey wrench Janey had used on me all those years ago. I bent to pick it up with my good arm but overbalanced and fell, grabbing the wrench as I did and rolling over to my side in a gymnastic move that would've surprised Mrs Simpson, our old PE teacher. But it left me on the floor. Suddenly Janey was stood astride me, swinging the gun down in an arc, aiming for my head. It was all I could do to hold the wrench up horizontally in both hands to deflect the clanking blow as it came. The vibration raced up my arm and the pain was unbelievable, as if she'd tried to wrestle my shoulder out if its socket. Once again she raised the gun above her head and with a victorious cry for what she knew would be the killing blow, she swung down again. I knew I couldn't defend myself as I had – my injured arm lay at my side like a dead weight– and in my anger, my desperation I flung the wrench at Janey, like an Apache throwing an axe in an old Western, the wrench flew from my hand, turning on its axis as it closed on Janey, the head smashing into her nose and caving in her upper jaw. Her arms dropped as the strength drained from her, buckling under the weight of the gun. A high-pitched moan escaped her lips, but still she continued to fight, staggering forward, aiming a kick at me on the ground like she had at Sal, as blood poured down her face and dripped all around us. I reached up and grabbed a handful of her shirt and yanked as hard as I could. Already unbalanced she fell forwards, tripping over Sal's immobilised form, her momentum carrying her towards the fire.

'Noooooo!' she screamed, finally letting go of the shotgun and putting her hand up to protect her face as the flames reached out and drew her in, wrapping themselves around her like the arms of a lover. The intense fire, still piled high with pallets, collapsed under her weight, sending flames, sparks and debris exploding out to the sides as she landed, writhing in the heat of the furnace, disappearing from view. Airborne sparks and embers hung around us, with more small exploding fireworks and I realised what was happening. The air was so charged with paraffin fumes where it had been poured on Sal, and where Janey had spilled it all around and on herself, and the flames of the fire were so hot as it spilled outwards that the whole area could go up, taking Sal and me with it.

Sal.

She was covered in fuel and very likely to be what would go up first.

'Sal,' I said to her, her knees still curled into her chest. 'We need to go, Sal. We need to go, now! Can you move, can you get up?'

'Fuck I don't know, she caught me a good one.'

'Well if you don't get up you're gonna end up like her.' More fireworks pinged off all around us as I bent and helped Sal to her feet. She was doubled over from where Janey had pulled the chains through from her arms behind her back, under her crotch to her front. Thankfully she hadn't chained her legs.

'Go, go, go,' I said, quickly ushering her away as the fire collapsed again and a shower of sparks crashed over where we'd just been standing.

As Janey collapsed on the unstable pallets in the fire, they fell backwards and flung her out the other side, completely ablaze. Her clothes and body burned in yellow and orange and red. She turned to look at me, opening her mouth which was just a raw blackened cavern, but no sound came out, reaching her hand up to point at me like Donald Sutherland in *Invasion of the Body Snatchers*. She ran at the cave entrance, flames streaming out behind her like afterburners on a plane, and either jumped down or fell into the hole, it was impossible to tell. Flames still poured out of the cave entrance for a few seconds, but then they died, leaving a plume of acrid smoke that continued to rise up for some time afterwards. We never saw Janey again.

'What goes around comes around,' I said, turning my attention once more to Sal. We walked round to where Katie and Clara were huddled together, the stench of paraffin strong on Katie's body.

'Don't go near the fire, for God's sake,' I said to her, my one arm dangling uselessly, blood dripping from my fingers.

'Thanks for that,' she replied pithily.

$$\infty \ \ \infty \ \ \infty$$

I heard sirens in the distance and looked up and saw the flashing glow of red and blue lights back in the village. It turned out that the residents of Newlands Farm Cottages had called the fire brigade when they'd seen the flames coming from the top lake over an hour before. A fire in the countryside wasn't a priority, but calls to the police reporting gun shots were, so we had a monopoly on the emergency services, the gravel around us soon becoming a parking area for police cars, fire engines and an ambulance. An armed response unit was the first on the scene, tooled up to the eyeballs with weapons and making us lay down on the ground. Given the extent of our injuries and being covered in paraffin, that wasn't going to happen, and it took us a few minutes to persuade them that we weren't the bad guys. A detective inspector came forward and began to talk to us and was soon despatching a car to Janey's house and ordering a forensic team. It was a long time before we could finally go back to The Wheatsheaf. Paramedics insisted on checking us over and patching us up. They wanted to take both Sal and me to hospital to be checked over. They said I needed any shot that hadn't gone straight through my shoulder to be removed, but we refused, so they glued the gash on my forehead from the monkey wrench and dressed my wounds. Then we were good to go.

The next few days saw rounds of interviews with various detectives, and we knew that the bungalow was being systematically pulled apart. I did go along to the hospital and had a small procedure to tidy my shoulder up. We never heard anything about the cave by the top lake, or Janey's body. The police were very cagey about it, as if they were embarrassed to discuss this aspect of the case, when they were keeping us informed about everything else. Asking separately we got the impression that they hadn't found her – but that was impossible, there was no way out – even the stagnant pool wasn't an escape route. Or was it?

∞ ∞ ∞

The police found a series of journals on Janey's bookshelves, which she'd started at the age of eight. Early ones were just inane scribbling, but their narrative coalesced as she got older into a conversation between her and someone else, occasionally named as Will. We found out that her parents had taken her to the family doctor when she was nine, concerned that she appeared to be having conversations with someone who wasn't there. The doctor dismissed this as an 'imaginary friend' even though she was a bit old, really. They assumed she'd grow out of it.

We could finally drift home and try to move on, although we were reunited at times by inquests and investigations. Beyond her parents, Mrs Grimshaw, Todd, Mr Grissholm and Luke Lewis, Janey was implicated in the deaths of fifteen other people, with another twelve having her hallmark but no evidence. It turned out that the rumours of other missing children, back in 1985, had been just that – rumours, caused by Luke Lewis' disappearance.

If anything good can be said to have come out of this whole nightmare, it was that the four of us stayed in touch. Not getting together very often after Janey's case was closed, but chatting continually on social media as we formed new relationships with each other. We also got to know a wider group, people we'd grown up with. Ironically it was as Janey had said, those that stayed local struggled – with their health, their happiness, jobs, businesses – and an alarming number died young, from cancers or neurological diseases.

Maybe she was right. Maybe you had to leave Laurendon to thrive, to succeed and be happy, and by staying around you condemned yourself to being dragged down with the rest of the village. Or maybe it wasn't the village itself that had gone bad. Maybe it was the other way around, and the one thing, the one person, who could truly call Laurendon home had cast his own spell over the place, haunting it, possessing it, treating the inhabitants like pawns in a game.

Maybe the one person defining all of Laurendon's history was the Shadow Man.

The End
Mark Brownless
January 2019

Author's Note

In thinking about being a kid and riding around my home village, on which Laurendon is based, but is actually a nice little village and not the despair ridden shithole that I've portrayed, it struck me how layered memories could be. I was trying to remember things from back in 1985 and when something would come to me, a whole load more things would unveil themselves. This became the essence of The Shadow Man – how memories are stored in the brain, and how, by peeling back one layer, more and more layers are brought to the fore – things that we'd long thought forgotten or would've thought we'd never remember again.

I read somewhere that, with the right training, the brain can remember every single thing it has experienced – we just aren't very well trained in storing and cataloguing those memories.

In the 1980s there really was a weekly magazine in the UK called 'The Unexplained.' And for £1.99 you could feast your eyes on UFOs, Nessie, Bigfoot and a whole host of other strange subjects, one of which was spontaneous human combustion. As Clara says in the book, it really was like 'nerd-porn' for a teenager like me who was slap bang in the middle of their target demographic. Seeing pictures of people's bodies completely burned to ash while their limbs remained intact seemed more bizarre and frightening than if there'd been nothing left of them. The idea that someone could just burst into flames in the comfort of their own home was more scary than the idea of being abducted by aliens or being attacked by a mythical monster. Clearly it still resonates to some degree or another.

Researching the more modern scientific theories about this particularly rare phenomenon has demystified it to a great extent. Explainable or not, however, the idea of one's own body consuming itself in flames is still a particularly disturbing thought.

And so developed The Shadow Man, a story that asks what is real and what isn't; such as memories that are either wrong or so incomplete as to effectively mean they are a lie, of people who've burned to death either because of spontaneous human combustion or more sinister means, and of terrible acts committed either by a vengeful ancient spirit or an impressionable disturbed youngster.

But what of us? How sure can we be that the memories we have are a true and accurate reflection of what has happened in our lifetime? How do we know that the life we've lived is the one that we remember? What if our brains are hiding something?

Memories. You can't trust 'em.

Acknowledgements

Talk about the difficult second album.

The idea for The Shadow Man came to me after I'd read C J Tudor's wonderful 'The Chalk Man.' And before you start getting concerned, apart from having 'The' and 'Man' in the title, they are very different stories. It was C J who got me thinking about childhood and riding round on our bikes in our village and started off the whole false memories idea, so I really must thank her for that.

The book wrote itself very very quickly, but actually stitching it together with the two timelines of 1985 and now was a different story, and I need to thank my editor, Jackie Bates, for all her help with that process and getting the finished book in your hands.

Making connections and networking is a hugely important part of the self-publishing industry, and over the last year I've had help and advice from Dave Chesson, Risa Fey, Tom Hunter-Hybert, Mo Jo Joiner, Nick Jones, Kevin Maguire, Stu Turton, Keith Wheeler and a great many others. Thank you to one and all.

Two people have been the 'glue' holding my self-publishing career together, and they are Sam Missingham and Dale L Roberts, who've both, rather foolishly, said they believed in what I do, and now they'll never be rid of me!

I'm very proud of the cover of The Shadow Man, and the eerie blue picture that has struck a chord with so many people. The credit for the picture goes entirely to photographer Mikko Karskela who can be found on Pixabay (https://pixabay.com/users/finmiki-5724486/). He's an incredibly talented guy and I feel so lucky to have found him and his pictures – thank you, my friend.

And finally, once more, to you dear reader. Thank you for reading, I hope you enjoyed Flip's story, and I hope we can be having this conversation, once again, at the end of another journey.

Contact Mark on social media, at:

www.markbrownless.com

www.facebook.com/markbrownlessauthor/

twitter.com/MarkBrownless

SIGN UP TO THE NEWSLETTER AT
www.markbrownless.com
AND GET

LOCKSLEY
A ROBIN HOOD STORY

MARK'S NEW SERIAL FICTION

FREE!

WHY NOT LEAVE A REVIEW AT AMAZON?

Printed by Amazon Italia Logistica S.r.l.
Torrazza Piemonte (TO), Italy

16476449R00150